ARIZONA KISS

Also by Ray Ring

Telluride Smile
Peregrine Dream

ARIZONA KISS

Ray Ring

LITTLE, BROWN AND COMPANY
BOSTON   TORONTO   LONDON

First Edition

The characters and events in this book are fictitious.
Any similarity to real persons, living or dead,
is coincidental and not intended by the author.

Library of Congress Cataloging-in-Publication Data

Ring, Raymond H.
    Arizona kiss / Ray Ring.
            p.   cm.
    ISBN 0-316-74656-8
    I. Title.
    PS3568.I567A88   1991
    813'.54 — dc20   90-25985

10   9   8   7   6   5   4   3   2   1

RRD VA

*Published simultaneously in Canada
by Little, Brown & Company (Canada) Limited*

Printed in the United States of America

To James M. Cain and,
defined by their state of mind, all the Arizonans

ARIZONA KISS

1

I DIDN'T SET OUT to kill anyone. All I wanted was a good story, which is all a journalist ever wants, but I should have seen it was going bad. Even on the drive up to the mine, even that early, there was a sign. One of those little omens. The idiot light flashed red on the dashboard: HOT, and I got a sweet whiff of antifreeze starting to boil. My damn car was punking out — that should have told me something. I could have turned back right then and there, nobody at the paper would have blamed me. I could have held off for a day or two, and who knows, the rest of it might have worked out differently. But all I did was keep my foot on the gas. And curse. That was my style.

I cursed the car and I cursed my idea of a job and I cursed all of Arizona for the umpteenth time. Of course the air conditioner was broken, nothing works anymore, and I was sopping in sweat. Staring at that little red light. HOT. Christ, was it ever. I had the windows down and the wind was cooking me. The two-lane patched blacktop, the dull hills that could grow only cactus and mesquite — all of it was suffering under the mean Arizona sun. The HOT light got redder and redder. I thought it was good luck that nothing blew before the top of the long grade. Three miles of coast-

ing got me down to the river, or what was left of it after the
smelter was through. Down a dirt turnoff I tried to blend in
with traffic for the mine: jacked-up pickups, beaten sedans,
vans decorated with the laughable landscape decals, all
crowded with people who were working their lives away
underground.

At the mine gate two guards in sweaty uniforms hung
back in the shade of their shack. Past them was a dirt lot
kicked up by a dust devil, and a concrete blockhouse dug
into the hill. Park and spit through the dust, shuffle into the
blockhouse — that was the routine. I carried a lunch box just
like the others did. Nobody asked me what the hell I was
doing. We clanged down a set of iron-mesh stairs. At the
bottom was the locker room where the morning shift was
coming off, yelling and horsing around and lining up naked
for the showers. I was coming in with the second shift and we
had nothing to celebrate. My locker took some finding and
the combination I'd been given didn't work until the third
try. Now I was getting some stares. Inside the locker was a
dinged-up hard hat and safety glasses, some other gear, and a
knotted rope that fed through a slot in the top and doubled
around a hook on a ceiling beam to end in a canopy of muddy
clothes. Anything worn underground had to be hung up
overhead, or the whole locker room would've been mud. I
lowered the bundle that had been left for me and peeled away
the parts — sweatshirt and coveralls and heavy rubber
boots — and tugged them on. They almost fit. I watched the
others and got ready like they did, belted on the little self-
rescuer, the can of factory air that, in a fire or cave-in underground, would be good for five minutes of desperation. I took
my lunch box and stamped clumsy steps into the lamp room,
rigged a lamp on my hard hat, the cable snaking down to a
battery on my belt. I could pass for a miner.

"Don't they charge these batteries anymore? What the hell."

"Chipmunks on the generator must've got tired."

"Fucking company."

The ones sniffing at me had decided to mind their own business and see what developed. It stayed ticklish in the line they formed to hand in their brass — the little tags that tell one miner from the next once they're covered in mud. I handed the brass I was using to the timekeeper and, poker-faced, he slapped it into a slot on the big board behind him. That was how they kept track of who was underground and who made it out at the end of each shift, and who didn't.

We took more iron stairs down and out the back way to another flattened patch of dirt where the hoist towers squatted over the shafts. Beyond the dirt a square mile of desert had been ruined. The ground had sagged and cracked and collapsed as the ore was dug out underneath. Under our boots were hundreds of miles of tunnels and shafts, copper, gold, silver, moly — the San Ignacio mine. Down there was a story.

"Momma, don't let your babies grow up to be miners."

"Willie Nelson you ain't."

"And he ain't me. He couldn't take it."

A whistle blew the signal to go underground. I thought I deserved a last look around. Turkey buzzards floated on thermals above the cracked ground. On the horizon pink mountains made jagged teeth. It would've made a photo, the usual one.

"Looks like sunset'll be worth seeing."

"We'll never know. No view from where we'll be."

"You saw it go down last Saturday, didn't you?"

"I worked O.T. Saturday."

"Then quit complaining."

The cage was a rusted iron box dangling inside the Num-

ber Three hoist, trembling on its cable as we got in and
packed tight. The cage man had a reefer leaf inked on his
hard hat. He slammed shut the mesh door and yanked a cord
and the cage lurched and began to sink. The ground rose up
and blocked the sky, and then all we had to look at was the
brown rock slipping by, and markers telling how many hundreds and then thousands of feet we were down.

The miners got louder the deeper we went. They whistled and cursed and yelled insults at the company and the
bosses. They pounded their lunch boxes against the iron
walls and shook the cage — stretching my nerve.

"Strike. Strike. Strike. Strike."

They cut it off as the cage settled roughly at the level
marked 2775. The cage man banged open the door and as
most of them unloaded so did I — safer to stick with the
crowd for a while. We switched on our lamps. Close all
around was the rock, chiseled and glistening and seeming to
radiate heat. Ice vests — hadn't some source told me that's
what they wore in the deepest hottest recesses down here?
Rubber-lined canvas vests packed with ice cubes — no Arizona gentleman should be without one. I hadn't stopped
sweating. Walking was a chore in the puddles and muck.

"This goddamn mine."

"Twelve bucks an hour for this."

"New hires coming on at seven and a half."

"New whores, you mean."

"We'll all be marked down if this keeps up."

"Fucking company."

We slogged along to the man-train, a string of dented ore
cars that had planks wedged in as seats, towed by an electric
locomotive the size of an old Cadillac. I swung aboard and
the locomotive groaned and fried the air. Then we were
jolting through the tunnels on the mainline. Timbers fanned

by. We passed one turnoff after another, sidetunnels where
ore could be loaded. Some fool was pissing in the watery
ditch beside the rails, and he nearly got clipped.

"He about lost it there."

"Hey, you moron! Hang it out somewheres else."

"What're those spots? I think you caught a few drops."

Then a slamming right off the mainline, straight, a left,
straight, another left. We rumbled to a stop and I hopped off
with a fragment of the crowd. The train rumbled on. The
others started into the sidetunnel and I lagged behind and
switched off my lamp. They didn't look back. Their little
circle of light got smaller and their talk dwindled away. Then
it was dark.

Blasting somewhere far off thudded softly, faint gusts
against my face. A single lamp bobbed my way from the
mainline — a boss, most likely, and that might mean questions. There was a wooden ladder fastened to the wall and I
felt my way up it to a beam where I could hunch in under the
rock. The lamp bobbed closer and went by below me and
then everything was black again. I waited. The last thing I
wanted was to be caught down here.

I gave it a hundred count and switched on my light and
opened my lunch box and lifted out the sandwich and can of
soda and paper towels. Underneath in a plastic bag was what I
needed to do my job: the little camera set up for dim light,
the rolls of extrafast film, the flash. And a map of the mine —
a puzzle of levels and tunnels and shafts, with certain things
marked. I jumped down when it looked clear.

The rest of the shift I slogged around underground, dodg-
ing miners and bosses and running off film. I got some good
shots: two derailments, one on a sidetrack and a bigger one
that made chaos on the mainline. Ore cars that had missing
taillights and broken couplers and shouldn't have been in

service. Tracks going bad, ties rotting and spikes lifting out and rails hardly parallel. Sagging electric lines, so many splices and frays it was a wonder the locomotives got any juice at all. The transformer room flooded six inches deep, and a sidetunnel blocked by rubble, where there'd been a cave-in the last shift that hadn't been cleaned up yet. A cabinet of explosives that was supposed to be locked and only the blastmaster had the key, except one of the doors had been ripped off and anything could be had. And the usual toxics in drums being stored where they shouldn't be stored and dumped where they shouldn't be dumped — stock shots anymore, as half the stuff made these days has to be handled like it's from another planet.

And I got some people shots: miners huddled under a light at the mouth of a sidetunnel, passing joints and cans of beer. More of them working in the Number Five shaft, inside the mesh with no safety belts and a thousand-foot drop. Plenty who were blowing off the regs about safety glasses or hard hats or antidust masks. And an engineer taking a hot shower of sparks, trying to muscle his locomotive's control arm back into contact with the overhead line. Another fool trying to piss against a train — it was an underground sport. A final stock shot, two bosses playing cards on an upended bucket.

Hiding out in a dead-end I stumbled across a hill of empty beercans, and shot that, and when I left the dead-end there was the capper: two miners sabotaging the mainline with crowbars, nice, giving me a sequence on the second derailment.

I shot it all and tried not to be noticed. I used the flash when I thought I could get away with it, and other times relied on existing light — the miners' lamps and the headlights on the locomotives and the bulbs spotted here and there in the tunnels. I wanted atmospheric stuff anyway. I

shot perspectives, looking deep into the tunnels, and way up
a shaft at the tiny mirage of daylight. I shot hordes and close-
ups of the giant cockroaches that were everywhere. And I
shot trains speeding over the fifteen-miles-an-hour limit,
slowing the shutter to make them a blur. I made one mistake
with the flash. A boss came prowling from somewhere and I
had to crawl underneath a parked ore car and play invisible
for a long five minutes.

At the end of the shift I repacked my lunch box and rode
the man-train with the miners to the Number Three shaft.
The cage man reeked of reefer.

"Hey man, get this cage moving."

"Take us out of this hole."

Of course there was a boss on board and he had to be
staring right at me. I was layered in mud like the others and
that helped. Going up, a couple hundred feet below the
surface we could smell the rain. A storm had moved in.
Nothing else makes the desert seem sweet.

The rain washed over us as we unloaded into the night and
swarmed into the blockhouse. I took back my brass from the
timekeeper and went through the locker-room routine,
hoisted my bundle of filthy clothes to the ceiling, ignored the
second round of stares and got out of there. I drove out the
gate with my evidence on the seat beside me, past two
guards who couldn't have cared less.

2

T HE NEWSROOM was down in Tucson, out south of the interstate, in what they call a campus-style industrial park. *News-Gazette* was scripted in lights on the building, which took up a square block behind clipped shrubs. A chemical stink hung over the parking lot, drifting in from the campus-style resins plant next door. That was one story we somehow never got around to. My parking space was number 94 according to the bronze slab bolted to the concrete log. Anybody who lasts ten years on the paper rates a personalized log, with a nameplate instead of a number. I didn't plan on sticking around for the honor. Not for what I made a week. Not considering what I had to put up with. Pretty soon I was going to get onto a bigger paper that paid some real money and swung some real weight. Yeah, pretty soon.

The TV cameras by the back door looked me over. "Macky," I said, held up my ID, and got buzzed on through.

All the papers in Arizona suddenly got uptight a couple years back, after a reporter in Phoenix got blown up by a bomb under his car, right outside his own newsroom — that's how our readers file a complaint. A pack of journalists rushed in from around the country vowing to investigate under every

rock and cactus patch until they nailed the murderer, but of
course they never did solve it, nice try — and now each year
there's a banquet in Phoenix and they give out an award
named after the dead man. It's something for every journalist
in Arizona to strive for, that award. And the newsrooms are
set up like fortresses.

Upstairs the night city desk was on deadline for the morning edition, phones ringing, terminals humming, reporters
and editors tapping out little stories. Rissler had stayed late
and was running the desk. He slapped down his phone and
jumped me.

"How'd it go? Any trouble getting in?"

"I guess not. Nobody made me."

He held out his palm and I had to give him five.

"Give me something to look at as quick as you can."

It wasn't even safe back in photo. Suzy Kino was there,
loaded down with her camera bag and gear, hesitating when
she saw me. "Rissler's been antsy all day. What are you two
up to?"

"It'll be out soon."

"I thought I'd earned the security clearance." Then she
tried to lighten up. "I've got a hot one. Another grip and grin.
Somebody's getting a plaque."

She took off and I had the shop to myself. I souped my
film and glassed the negatives, starting printing the likelies
in the darkroom. They came up lively in the trays.

The prints had a look: grainy and harsh, black-and-
whites, no shadings, every trace of light a cut in the darkness. Images from underground. They would tell my story.
They were strong enough to stand alone, with as few words as
possible on the page, just a minimum of context, nothing to
tire the so-called readers.

Words are a fine old tradition in the news business but

they're cholesterol anymore. I should know, I started out in words, as a reporter, and switched over to pictures when I saw where the world was headed. Now I can shoot just about anything anywhere, no matter what the conditions, and when I'm on a story I get it in pictures and the readers like it that way. It won't be long before even a string of writing like what I'm putting down here will be a relic, and nobody will be able to string three thoughts together, but there'll still be plenty of stories told in pictures, instant stories that hit hard, then on to the next.

I was working up the derailment sequence when Rissler pushed through the lighttight door.

"What've we got?"

"Take a look on the dryer."

Jack Rissler was the only one at the paper who knew what I was up to most of the time. He backed me, and I needed that, but I didn't need to be his buddy and I didn't need him horning in on my story. He had a habit of taking over the big ones just as they were breaking. Poring over my shots from underground, he got excited like he always did, biting his lips, scratching his mustache, bulging his eyes, doing his own narration, working himself into my story until he could believe it had happened to him as much as to me.

"Great stuff. We've got guys wrecking the tracks. And the train going off. What a mess. Some guy toking up? It's a party. Whoopee. A mountain of beercans — Coors, no less. Very untidy. These drums — hazardous markings? Pretty careless with this shit. And the bosses playing cards. Perfect. And sparks, we've got sparks burning this poor guy. A little behind on maintenance I'd say, like years behind. We've got guys standing around, what?"

"In the shaft. No safety belts."

"That's a boss with them? Very good."

Rissler went on like that until he had the details.

"They'll be after you when we put these out with your credit. Photos by Macky. They'll be after your ass."

"They'll want it to die down quick."

"We'll keep it going." Rissler was like me, always on the lookout for a story he could ride. That's the way to get ahead in the news business, riding a big story. I just didn't want him riding mine.

"Tomorrow you talk to the lawyers," Rissler said.

"You know what they'll say: Don't say anything."

"Yeah. Just let them know we might be hit with something. Trespassing, invasion of privacy. Macky's been busy."

He held out his palm, and I had to give him five again.

"You've got mud behind your ear," he said. "That one."

I drove home to the little guest house where I lived. They call them guest houses, but of course they aren't big enough for any guests. Just one room with a sofa and a table and a bookcase and a bed against the other wall, and closet-size kitchen and bath. At least with a place that small, any kind of cooler does the job. I cranked it on and opened the windows so the curtains were flapping, and looked at my three potted cactus. They still looked dead. Cactus can survive just about anything, but mine had shriveled and turned black — I'd given them too much attention or not enough. One was just a husk and broke off when I touched it. I wasted some water on them and my housekeeping was done. I paced the perimeter of the little room and got irritated at the stuff I'd been carrying around in my pockets, the just about worthless coins and gas station charge card receipts that I always intended to check against the monthly bill, but never did. The bulk of it was clips, off the wires or generated by Tucson and Phoenix papers, that I was saving for my Arizona file, with the usual headlines summing up the angles: Sunny Arizona leads the country in skin cancer. Arizona at the bottom for high-school graduation rates. Arizona number one in car wrecks and insurance-company gouging. Arizona the land of wide-open spaces making its move as a drug-smuggling corridor and dump for bodies done execution-style. I tucked them away in the manila folder that was already bulging with other Arizona news I'd archived, all the neat journalistic studies showing we're roughly worst in water supplies and voter registration and pay scales and health care for the poor or crazy and so on, and tops in everything from allergies to bankruptcies to senior-citizen suicides and venomous reptiles and horny toads. I was still snorting over the evidence when Suzy Kino showed up.

"I came, they gripped and grinned, I shot." She gave herself a handshake, imitating the ceremony where somebody had gotten a plaque. Like most of them just starting out in newspapers, fresh-faced and scrubbed and college-educated in How To Be Hip 101, she had to act like a veteran. She had to use all the lingo and swagger around in a safari vest, her pockets bulging with film and lenses and supplies. She had to attach herself to me. That part, and how she was one of those hired on the basis of blue eyes and clipped blond hair and no obvious flaws, I hadn't minded at first.

"I brought in the mail," she said. She had a stack wedged under her arm. "The box was crammed full. It's that black aluminum thing on the wall outside the door."

"Put it with the rest."

She dropped it on the bigger stack on the floor in the corner. "Could be something important in there. Like a coupon for an attitude transplant."

"I've heard that one."

"That's what I mean. You're so cute — you and your stash

of bad news." She ran her fingers through her hair, she was used to that working for her, but it just put me more on edge. "With your nose in that, you finish whatever important job was taking all your time?"

"For tonight."

She tried to kiss me, and I avoided it. "Macky, you're fading on me."

"You don't have to be so bright-eyed about everything."

"Some nights you didn't mind."

"It's caught up to me."

"Come on. Nobody's this burned out."

"You know something about grip and grin?" I gripped her, the way she'd liked it before, but didn't want it then, and that's why I did it. I grinned. She broke away.

I told her, "Nothing lasts in this business. Everything we do folds into a little envelope and in a year it's turning yellow and breaking apart on the creases."

"You keep that line ready, don't you? You're the best shooter on the paper but I should've been telling you what a shitheel you are. That's what you want."

"Welcome to the world."

"You've managed to make me feel sweet and boring."

I said, for her benefit more than mine, "We're communicating now."

By morning Rissler had assembled a team to put out the package: Max Durazo to do the layout and Harry Fulton the mining reporter to snipe and complain about the raid on his beat and Doris from promotion and somebody else from the back shop to say there was no way to rush into print. Rissler buddied up with all of them and got them into line and said we were coming out with an eight-page special section the next day — just before the miners went on strike.

"When is it they walk out?" Rissler asked.

Rissler already knew the strike deadline was midnight Thursday, he and I'd talked about it enough, but he was trying to include Harry, and make out like we were relying on Harry's great expertise, which came from tapping out little stories based on company press releases and quarter-cent drops in the price of copper in Chile.

"Midnight Thursday," Harry said.

"Any chance they'll call it off?"

"The unions backed themselves into a corner. They'll have to stay out a month anyway, or they'll look like wimps."

"No chance the company will settle?"

"Check your calendar," Harry said. "It's 1991."

Then we had to look at the photos, and pick out the ones to use. Overnight they hadn't lost any impact. Spread on the conference table, they were an indictment of a killer mine. More dead and injured were being hauled out of the San Ignacio than any other mine in the country. These shots would show why, and they wouldn't allow any argument.

This wouldn't be the kind of sorry, he-said she-said journalism where charges are made and denied and the reader is left wondering. No, when these shots hit the street, people would be nailed. The bosses would be nailed for neglecting the equipment and risking anything for production and profits. The miners would be nailed for blowing off safety regs and sabotaging the rail-line and declaring general anarchy — trying to make their situation look worse before the strike or just raising hell, it didn't matter. And as usual, the government agencies would be nailed for everything. Everybody would be nailed — the mark of a good story. That's the real purpose of journalism, that's why it rates up there in the constitution and the courts, because it's the only tool with which certain people can be nailed. Every journalist has a high-sounding rap, and that's mine.

The only question that hung us up was what to call the package — anything out of the ordinary needs a logo and a snappy standing head. Rissler thought something like *The Trouble Underground* or *San Ignacio Blues*. Harry wanted *Mining: The Hardest Job*, which prompted Max to suggest *Snapshots from Hell*. Doris said profanity might affect rack sales.

"Does that mean we'll sell more papers?" Rissler asked.

"It could go either way," Doris said. "But there'll be complaints."

"Goodness, then we better not," Rissler said. I laughed. "What do you think, Macky?"

"If *Snapshots from Hell* is out, I like *San Ignacio Blues*."

"Not too ethnic, is it?"

"You thought of it, Rissler, you're white," Max said.

"Let's go with it then. Get some rack cards printed up and put a promo on top of page one. Macky, you want a mug shot inside to go along with the credit?"

"No. The more people know what I look like, the less fun I can have."

"That's what I thought. Max, get a line sketch of Macky out of the art department, make sure it doesn't look too much like him. Make him ruggedly handsome. *San Ignacio Blues* is a one-man photo spread, and we better give the readers some indication of who's behind it. It'll give the section an identity."

I laughed again, loudly.

"Tell the art department to make him bald and fat," Rissler said. He held out his palm and Max had to give him five. Then he walked off full of purpose, probably headed to the john.

"Now there's a story," Max said.

"He's all right," Doris said. "You get that way in this business."

"Who does?" Max said. "The same to you."

Rissler didn't seem to understand how he came off with the low-fives and all the rest, trying to be buddies with everybody from the lowest library clerk to the publisher's wife, especially the publisher's wife. The high-powered managing editor who somehow still managed to be human, that was his act. Nobody was fooled. Like how he always left his suit coat draped over his chair and went around in a rumpled shirt with the sleeves rolled back and his tie yanked loose, as if he didn't give a damn about how he looked, only it was obvious he did, because he never looked any different and everything he wore was top label. And how he had his receding curls styled once a week to look slightly untended, and how his little mustache grew wild but never made it past the ends of his lips because he shaved around it so meticulously. That was Rissler, all tied up in himself and trying to act just the opposite. It could be he knew exactly what he was doing, and figured that anyone who didn't call him on it was already intimidated. It could have been his little test.

He didn't bother me the rest of the day while I worked up the copy to go with the photos. I kept it simple, just an explanation of each shot, and then the stats on arms broken and legs severed and bodies crushed per month at the San Ignacio mine. I needed the most current totals so I called Hank Boswell, the company flak. He was in charge of passing out their lies to the press.

"How you doing?" Boswell said, and that was lie one. I was the last person he wanted on his back. I'd already nailed him and the company once, on smelter emissions — they'd been puffing all out on nights when the wind took the smoke away from the pollution monitors. I'd gotten a nice shot of the full moon just about blotted out by this big pale sick-looking sulfur cloud coming out of the stacks. The company had been subjected to a real Arizona crackdown — they had to pay a token fine and promise not to do it again. Of course they still did, but not around the full moon, so photos were more difficult and I hadn't been able to follow up yet. Boswell downplayed the toll underground.

"Unfortunate accidents that could happen anywhere, on any industrial job site." That was Boswell's rap. "The company is concerned. The safety department gives lectures."

I made sympathetic noises and ticked off my questions. I caught him in a couple more lies, how heart attacks underground were listed, that sort of thing, and managed to jack him up over the most recent totals we had.

"What's this for?" Boswell asked. "You got something coming out?"

"We might be putting something together."

"When might I see it?"

"Tomorrow, maybe."

"Nice talking to you," Boswell said, and hung up. He wasn't as bad as some of them. His lies were just the company's lies. Handing them out was his job.

3

THE COMPETITION, the other papers and the TV stations and the poor bastards in radio, had to follow our lead on the *San Ignacio Blues*, and they had to play it tough for once. Within hours after we hit the street they were swarming the company and the miners and unions and us for comment. If the same story had been done in words it would have been played a lot softer, and it would have been a lot easier to ignore. But my photos were right under Arizona's nose. Half the state was trying to call up the newsroom that morning, and of course Rissler was prancing around.

"The wires have picked it up. Nobody can report anything without giving us first mention. I love it. Harry, I want twenty-five inches on the company's stance for tomorrow. Get the unions in there too, and whether the strike is affected. And some quotes high up from some mine-safety guys saying how this is something worth looking into and it's a good thing we did. And a sidebar on how wide the story gets around, who's picked it up, and how we started it so nobody forgets."

"How about a quote from Macky's mom?"

"Just get on it. Macky? How's our man taking it?"

"Our man? You mean my man."

"You know who I mean. You talked to him yet? Make sure we're okay in case this thing gets to court."

"Rissler! Oh-three's for you. Channel Twelve wants to come down and get some footage of the newsroom, and somebody to defend the section."

"Defend it, hell. That's on oh-three?"

I got out of there and drove out to see my man — my contact at the San Ignacio mine. Jimmy Santos. He'd gotten me in, loaned me his locker and his filthy clothes and hard hat and his brass and other gear and given me a lesson on how to sneak underground. He'd done it for the same reason anyone helps a journalist — to settle a score.

Santos was a third-generation miner. His grandfather had worked his last shift at San Ignacio and gone home to cough himself to death back before they had any regulations on how much of the company's dust a man was expected to breathe. Then his father had been crushed by a cave-in. That didn't stop Santos from signing up at the mine right out of high school. That was all his people knew, that was the life they felt locked into. I'd met him in a miners' bar one night when I was out shooting pool and working sources. He used me to carry on his little guerrilla war.

He'd tipped me about the midnight pollution at the San Ignacio smelter, and other company embarrassments that couldn't be done in pictures, and I'd passed them along to the reporters. I kept his name out of it and in return he got revenge, justice, whatever word you prefer — and at least as important, the idea that he made a difference in the world.

I had sources like him in all sorts of positions, from the mayor's office to the local missile plant, and they all had the same motivations. They all felt stepped on, by the bosses or the gods. They all enjoyed the sense of power that came from dealing with a reporter on the sly, the feeling they could jack around their whole company or organization just by whispering a few secrets or shooting a pilfered memo or two in my direction. They got off on the intrigue. And there was usually a speck of real dirt in even their wildest allegations. I didn't mind settling their scores and pumping them up so long as I got a good story out of it. In the news business, you're nothing without your sources.

Santos lived in one of the fifty or hundred subdivisions called Sunset Ridge that have been built in the last year or so to accommodate all the people that have to move to Arizona because where they come from is even worse. By the entrance they had the stringers of plastic flags snapping in the breeze. From there on it was nothing but one-story starter homes of chicken-wire and stucco. I stopped across from 3345 Sunset Lane. Three feet of bare dirt on each side separated it from starter homes numbers 3343 and 3347. Probably it looked better at sunset. Santos took his time answering my knock, and when he did, he had a tire iron ready to swing.

"I just about give up on you," he said. "You're about a day late, man." He opened the door wider and let me see the fresh fiberglass cast that wrapped his left arm from shoulder to wrist.

"Shit, Santos."

Moving stiffly, he closed and locked the door and leaned the tire iron in the corner. The cast had a ninety-degree bend that made him look ready to throw a left jab. He tended to give that impression anyway. He was a little pug, stocky with thick arms and legs, and an unlined face that never smiled.

"You're lucky Lupe isn't here. She don't want you in the house anymore, man. She don't even want me talking to you."

He moved himself into the kitchen and worked two beer bottles out of the fridge, using his good hand.

"I said to her, you didn't break my arm. It was those two guys who got me down right in my own front yard at five this morning. It took a couple of them to do it. I answer the door still half asleep and they drag me out in my fucking underwear."

"Who was it? Anybody you recognize?"

"Fuck no." He passed me the beers and I twisted the caps and we finished the routine. "Company assholes or union assholes or just freelance assholes. I figure they had time to see the paper and jump in their truck and come over here."

"What kind of truck?"

"Forget it, man."

"They say anything?"

"Just for me not to have nothing to do with you anymore. I said, with who? And that's when they broke it. I could hear the bones go. Lupe came out screaming at them and they took off."

"You call the cops?"

"Double fuck no. And say what? I sneaked you underground and somebody didn't like it? They'd be the last ones I'd call. If I wanted to make something out of it I'd just get my cousins and we'd run down these guys and kick some ass."

"What about the hospital?"

"I fell off a ladder. I got up early to work on the cooler."

"They believe it?"

"They believe I'm a dumb Mexican or a lying Mexican and they don't care."

"How do you suppose these assholes got onto you?"

"You dress out of my locker, use my brass, you think

everybody around you is blind or what? Maybe they didn't
know who you were, but they sure could see you weren't me
and you were up to something. They didn't give a shit until
they had a reason to, that's all."

Outside a noise got louder and then rapped away: a car
with an exhaust leak. Santos tracked it.

"Last time I'll try anything that loco," he said.

We stood there in the little kitchen. It had a stainless-
steel sink and a dishwasher and the stamped-out cabinets and
the cottage-cheese ceiling. Santos moved over to the sink
and looked out the tiny window at the plot of dirt that was his
backyard.

"I saw the paper. You got some pretty good pictures. *San
Ignacio Blues.* That's pretty good too. They should make a
song out of it. Nine years I been working in that mine. You
know how many times I come close to eating it? That place
killed my grandfather and my father and now it's trying to kill
me. So don't give me any crap about what I should be doing
now. Man, you don't know a damn thing about it."

"I'm not giving you any crap."

"You already did. It was your loco idea."

"I'm sorry your arm got broken, Santos."

He slapped the cast. "I don't give a fuck about this. It'll
heal. I'll be back at work when the strike's done. I just been
thinking. I got a family. I got a house. I got a job and so what
if it sucks? Every job sucks. I need that paycheck."

"Lupe help you with all this thinking?"

"She's pregnant, man. We're having a baby."

He had me there. He was all tied up in the streamers
down the block, with a baby on the way. Nothing ties you up
faster or tighter than a baby. "Congratulations."

"We just got to cool it for a while."

"Okay, then we'll cool it. Anybody else wants to make

anything out of me going underground, our lawyers will take care of it."

"Your lawyers couldn't do shit for me this morning. Not unless they knew kung fu. Lawyers won't enter into it. Won't be any court case. Won't be no miners being witnesses."

"So everybody will cool it. You can raise that baby and send it off to work underground and your grandson and great-grandson. They can all cool it . . . Every time that arm aches, you're going to want to kick some ass. Just remember how much we kicked in this morning's paper."

A car pulled in the driveway. Lupe came in. Her face had the lines.

"What are you doing here?" she demanded. She cursed in Spanish and yanked open a drawer to grab a carving knife and came at me, stabbing low for punctuation.

"All these years he's been telling you things and you put them in the paper and look good. Only when somebody's got a problem they come to him, not you, and they snap his arm and maybe they want to do worse. You leave us alone. You got your story, now get out."

She chased me out to my car with her knife. It was a real Arizona good-bye, thanks for coming, see you soon and if I do you're dead, *chingadero*.

I tried to brush it off driving around and of course the HOT light came on and then steam and that awful knocking from under my hood. I had to put myself at the mercy of the nearest gas station. Bob was his name. It was spelled out in a little patch on his blue shirt. Bob popped the hood and decided I needed new hoses, a new radiator cap and a water pump, along with a thermostat. The usual pitch. You could pull in with a flat tire and they'd try to sell you a water pump.

"Bob," I said. "Conventional spelling? Put in the thermostat and start a game show with the rest."

He got it enough to let me alone, and do the job, and not
charge me more than twice what it was worth, and then I
drove to some bar where I had a Mexican beer and told the
bartender to keep his wedge of lime. That was how they were
drinking Mexican beer that year, as if they didn't like the
taste. I got tired of how empty the place was and of how I
looked in the mirror behind the bar, and how I was now
between stories.

Toward sunset I parked at the top of a big rock that poked
up in the middle of nowhere, looking out over miles of
stinking desert. The rock was maybe six hundred feet tall,
with a sheer face and a way up the back through some mined-
out hills on an old bulldozer road that wasn't as good as the
description sounds. The top of the rock was a place I went to
escape everything else, and for the rush. The spot of level
ground at the summit was littered with broken beer bottles
and the bones of campfires and a boom-box radio that had
been stomped on and broken into pieces. I had a shot of
tequila from the bottle I'd bought at a convenience store and
got my parachute pack out of the trunk and slipped it on, and
bundled the little pilot chute in one hand. I didn't walk to
the edge of the drop-off and look down. It's better when you
don't look, when you don't have the immediate knowledge
of what's coming. I took another shot of tequila and rested the
bottle on the car seat and started my run toward the low sun.
I ran faster straight for the drop-off, yelled and dived out into
nothingness.

Somebody watching would have thought it was suicide.
Maybe it was, and maybe it wasn't.

The rush. I fell, and fell, in a spread-eagle. Time disappeared. The wind tore at my ears and my face and clothes. My guts did their tricks. It was one long yell. I took it to the limit and a little past, and threw the pilot chute as the desert rose up to meet me. The pilot and then the main luffed out and jerked me vertical and I began to fall slower. I worked the strings to steer clear of the rock face and the cactus closer and closer below and hit the desert hard and rolled.

Yeah, oh yeah. You survived one more, Macky. The ankle's turned a little and the shoulders are sore, but you made it.

I wadded the chutes and noticed that the desert looked a little better. I laughed and started limping up the long trail to the car. On the trail after dark I was still feeling the rush.

That's what we do to unwind in Arizona — get some elevation and then aim ourselves at the desert with the only insurance a scrap of temperamental nylon. I'd done enough jumping out of perfectly good airplanes to understand anybody can manage that, it's so organized and rehearsed and safe according to the statistics. Jump off something anchored like the rock, or the skyscrapers and radio towers that other crazies use as launch points, and you get an honest to-hell-with-it rush. You have to really hurl yourself over the edge to fall clear — without the forward momentum of the airplane you're just falling straight down, all the sensations of an altitude jump packed into microseconds. You see exactly how fast you're plummeting with the rock face hurtling by, the pilot chute wadded in your hand because there's no time to deploy it from a backpack, and if it and the main pop right, you get on the strings to stay clear. One wrong breeze can turn you into a smear. There's no margin for mistakes with the desert below so close, and you never know how it's going to end, and until it does you're rushing, way out there where nobody else goes.

But the effects of the jump never last. They'd worn off by
the time I got home. I took the bottle inside and cranked on
the cooler and got into the tequila, straight. If it's any good,
and even if it isn't, that's the way it should be drunk. One
more night and there I was with the convenient tequila. I
started thinking, and that was a mistake. I thought about
Santos and Lupe and the knife. I thought about all the babies
that would someday go to work underground or in a newsroom. I thought about my story lighting up Arizona, and so
what, and Suzy Kino, and double so what, and all the people
who weren't there keeping me company and why they
weren't — and how my best conversations anymore were
with myself.

I thought about a world made up of people using each other
and how logical that made my business. Once I had seen it
differently. I chuckled at the memory and then didn't like the
sound of my chuckle or even the word. People wanted their
stories done and somebody to blame afterwards. People
wanted me to care and then not care. Switch on, do the story,
switch off, and don't be reluctant or they'll use the knife.
Again and again over the years I'd had to live each story in
snatches and get on to the next and what had that cost? And
just which particular story was one too many, Macky?

I had some more tequila and thought about the jump and
how each time I cut it closer, lost a little more altitude before
popping the chutes.

About the only thought I had that was any good at all was
that the phone was ringing and I didn't have to answer it. I
had the answering machine on and I could listen to the
recording of myself saying I wasn't home and then Rissler
leaving his message.

"Macky? You laggard. You're probably dancing right there
with señorita tequila. I've got everybody in the newsroom

fielding your calls all day and I can't put the paper out by myself. I'm switching your extension on call forward, over to this line. This is your public, you deal with it."

After that the phone kept ringing.

"Macky? I can't say who I am, but I work underground. It took a lot of balls to do what you did, and keep it up. You got it wrong about the unions, though."

"Macky? I've been a subscriber to the *News-Gazette* for twenty-three years and I've never seen anything like what I did today. Shocking. To think they let that go on. They ought to investigate the whole thing and vote in a Libertarian for once. That would clean it up."

"Macky? This is Hank Boswell at the San Ignacio. The company feels you've been a bit unfair. We'd like to set up a meeting to give our side of it. The least you could do is return my calls."

"Macky, you slimy spying ratfuck. How'd you like some acid thrown in your face?"

"Macky? This is Sergeant Glennon at the sheriff's department. You've photographed criminal acts such as drug use and criminal damage to property. The photos and the negatives are evidence that could be useful in prosecuting any suspects that can be identified. Call me right away."

"Macky? George Franks down at Channel Twelve news. There's been a charge made that you beat up a guy so you could take his place underground. Any comment?"

"Macky? Those were really some photos. My third-grade class would like you to come talk about how you did it."

Suzy Kino: "Macky? I'm not coming over until you invite me. Give me a call . . ."

Then back to: "Macky? It'll be hydrochloric acid. You won't be looking through a lens anymore once your eyes are burned out of your head, you miserable . . ."

"Macky? . . ."
"Macky? . . ."
"Macky? . . ."

I listened to all of it and worked my way through the tequila. The public be served. At ten o'clock I watched the TV news and what they did with it, which wasn't much, but more than what they did with most real stories. They led with blow-ups of some of my photos, and had snips of different people commenting for or against, and then Rissler doing his act, about how sometimes you had to go to extra lengths to get the meaningful stories, and how the paper stood by everything. I flicked around and the other stations had it about the same. None of them let it go on past two or three minutes.

I shut off the TV and opened the front door to make the place a little bigger, and looked at whatever was outside. The phone kept ringing. I could have shut it off, but the voices were keeping me company.

"Macky? . . ."
"Macky? . . ."

And then the one that counted. It didn't sound like much at first — a woman, unsure, her voice slurred and low, as if she was into some tequila herself. "Is anyone there? Hello? I won't leave my name. You probably can't handle it anyway."

She called back a minute later. "I should let you decide. You got into that mine. This would be more difficult. Somebody big could be brought down. Somebody . . . who needs it. You have to come out here so I can look you over. I won't give this to just anybody. It might be too much for you. I don't know. You come out here tomorrow morning and then we'll see."

She gave directions and hung up. She called back again. "I know you're not my kind of people. Nobody is my kind. But I think this is something you'll like. I wouldn't be calling you if I didn't think that. Because it's going to take commitment. You understand what I'm saying? Commitment."

She hung up again. The phone rang and I picked it up.

"Macky? Pure hydrochloric, you sneaking son of a bitch, a faceful of it . . . ."

She didn't try a fourth time, but she had gotten through to me with that stuff about commitment, and how nobody was her kind. She sounded like my kind.

4

S HE HAD A TRAILER planted in dust and scrub on a dirt road outside of town. It was one of those places where people end up. Arizona has a lot of them. The front steps were a pile of cinder blocks. The doorbell had been ripped out of its socket and the wires were dangling. When I banged on the door the louvers made the sound of a rattler about to strike. Cheaply reproduced rock-and-roll strained at me from inside. I had to bang for a while. "All right, all right," she said, and yanked it open.

At first scan she was some chippie: black-haired, brown-eyed and dusky, with Indian cheekbones and an old break in the bridge of her nose. Somebody must have smacked her there for looking too good and knowing it. She wasn't hiding much in the usual outfit: jogging shorts, a tank top, flip-flops on her feet, suitable for a night at the opera in Arizona. She knew just what she was doing balancing on the top step with one knee cocked, and I had to remind myself why I was there.

"Russell Macky?"

"Just make it Macky."

"Mind showing me some ID?"

I dug it out and handed it to her. She made a big deal out of inspecting the photo, then handed it back.

"It doesn't look like you."

She turned sideways so I had to brush by her going in. The succession of freeze-frames, I saw her as any shooter sees a subject: her in the doorway, cut diagonally by the harsh sunlight that flattened two-thirds of her face and just highlighted the rounded knob of her shoulder, the rest of her softened by shadow; the close-up of her eyes set in the cheekbones tracking me halfway through her turn; now in full shadow another close-up glancing down her chest, the intimate angle, framing the split of her breasts inside the gaping vee of the tank top, her abstract curves versus the machinemade electric-turquoise fabric; one more close-up before I was past, the inside half of her down to her shoulder, her complexion smooth and deep, the one eye wide open looking right up into mine, the half of her mouth turning upward at the corner in an almost imperceptible smile; then the final shot, looking out the door with her a dark silhouette against the brightness, the lines of her, her hip and elbow out so her arm defined a triangle of sunlight, something intriguing about how again she cocked herself.

She smelled of sweat. It was even hotter inside the trailer than it was outside. Those little boxes can really heat up. The air was dead, she didn't have a cooler or a fan going to move it around. Her hair hanging down in back was trapped inside the tank top, as if she'd just pulled it on.

She giggled for no reason I could identify, a little girl sound, and left the door open and came inside. She flip-flopped over to the rock-and-roll radio, fingered the volume knob, turned it louder while she looked at me. Then she switched it off. Flies buzzed around, big biting flies, not the kind that mean garbage, just the ones that let you know life in the country isn't any sweeter than anywhere else, no matter what they say.

"You want a drink?" She was back to her adult act.

"No thanks."

"So sit down."

I was stooping even though I didn't have to, trailers always make me feel like I'm barely fitting inside them. There was a couch made out of woven cane and cushions; it creaked but held up when I tried it. She leaned against the kitchen counter and crossed one leg over the other and reached up and lifted her hair out of the tank top. She was playing me, all right — that much I could enjoy from the beginning.

"I won't talk to anybody if I can't see his eyes."

I took off my sunglasses.

"That's better."

I could feel sweat on my face.

"He fights dogs," she said. "It's against the law."

"Who?"

"Pit bulls. Mean."

I didn't say anything.

"It should be worth something. I need cash. I got to get the cooler fixed."

I managed to study the carpet instead of her legs. It was the discount cut, lime shag that never looks clean. She flip-flopped over to the window where the cooler was jammed in, clicked the knobs around and got only a low moan. She wound up and slapped the front of the case, and did it again. The cooler thrummed and picked up speed. She stood facing it with her hands spread against the wall, fringes of her hair fanning out in the mechanical wind, and talked over her shoulder.

"It'll be good for five minutes now. Then you got to whack it again. Everything takes a whack in this heat. And we better get used to it. Ozone holes, the greenhouse effect —

we'll wake up one day and the whole world'll be as bad as this."

"Why don't you tell me who it is, and then we'll see if it's worth any money to the paper."

"Don't kid me. They got a policy or something against it. They don't pay for information, even when it's as good as this." She turned and let the cooler blow on her back. "I'm asking you, not the paper."

"Maybe I've got the same policy."

"You don't have any policies." She spit out the last. It had taken her a while, but she had gotten around to it.

She tossed a newspaper section down on the couch. *San Ignacio Blues*. "I've seen your work. You sneaked underground. Don't tell me about policies. You go right for the throat. That's why I called you."

"It's nice to be known."

"Not the way you are, maybe. So what about it? You willing to pay for a story?"

"I can't say until I know what it is." That was me playing her — I wouldn't pay, because I was going to get the story anyway. If she wanted to pretend the money was the reason she'd called me up, I wasn't going to be the spoiler.

"So I have to trust you. I told you on the phone it was something you'd like doing."

"I like it so far."

She smiled. Of course the cooler picked that moment to shudder and go off. She whirled and slapped it again, and nothing happened. She gave it another one, and still nothing.

"Sometimes you got to let it rest."

"Before this goes on too much longer I'm going to have to know why I had to come all the way out here."

"You know."

"Give me a name."

"Harker. Leo Aloysius Harker."

"The Judge?" Well, well. "Everybody knows he's got dogs. You saying he fights them? Can you prove it?"

"I can prove it. I want to show the world what he is."

"And what's that? What's your relationship with him?"

"My what?" She stood over me and yanked up her shirt. Her belly was fine, but vandalized by dark red smears — three of them, each about the size and color of my car's idiot light: HOT.

"If you call being somebody's ashtray a relationship, then that's what we got."

I was done looking at those burns. I got up and crowded her. Her breathing was ragged. Up close, with those cheekbones and dark eyes, her face looked like a skull.

"He puts me up in this dump. That's how it is." She didn't wait to see how I'd take it. She flip-flopped over to the fridge and got out an ice cube and rubbed the back of her neck.

"You want that drink now?"

"Ice water would be fine."

She fixed me up, with my own ice cube and all, and by then I was calmed down. The water tasted warm even with the ice. The Judge's water and the Judge's ice. She flip-flopped away and smacked the cooler again. Nothing.

"Damn."

I asked, "You'll help me nail him?"

She let me see some real emotion then. "I'll help you."

"I better know who you are, then."

"Nobody. Alice Malone."

I didn't say I was pleased to meet her. She didn't seem to mind. That's how we introduce ourselves in Arizona.

*   *   *

Maybe you're thinking I should have called somebody else in on it, some reporter to give me a hand, and to keep watch on her and me. That was the last thing I wanted to do, and not because of her. I told you, I liked to work alone, because then I could do it my way with no argument, and the right way too. Then the story and the credit were mine all the way. Anyway, most reporters only muddle everything up — they're nothing too sharp, their wits dulled by having to pretend that what the average citizen has to say is worth writing down. After a while most of them get to believing whatever they're told, which of course makes them useless on a real story.

But I did have to tell Rissler something. I needed his approval to spend time on it. I left out Alice Malone's legs and the burns on her belly. He got excited anyway.

"Think she's on the level?"

"I don't know. She giggled."

"She what?"

"Never mind. She says she can deliver the Judge, but she isn't giving us all of it. She has her own idea about how all this should work out. And I don't think she's as cheap as she wanted to come off. Almost, but not quite."

"Maybe you better check her out too."

"I plan on it."

"Think you can shoot some of these dogfights?"

"She says she can get me in."

"That's a tough crowd."

"Yeah."

"This could be the best yet. Debunking the Judge, that would send out some ripples. Take a couple of weeks. I'll see nobody bothers you. I'll get somebody else to do the follow-up on *San Ignacio Blues*. I know how much you hate follow-ups. We'll clean up your mess, after we've rubbed everyone

in it." Then I had to give him five. He was my buddy, for the
next couple of weeks anyway.

I pulled the clips on the Judge and Alice Malone. We had
nothing on her. On him we had an armful of envelopes
stuffed with stories, going back to when he graduated in law
at the university, and ending with his retirement two years
ago, concentrating on the six terms he'd served on the
Superior Court bench earning his reputation as simply the
Judge. Almost all of it was daily shorts, telling who got sent
away for how many years and what prosecutor or defense
attorney was trying to put over the most fantastic tale at the
moment — the usual stuff, nothing particularly hard-hitting
or more than half true.

There was one long feature done just before the Judge
retired where the reporter had gotten in his own digs. He
had the Judge sucking away on those black cigarillos every
minute he wasn't in court, and the Judge's bicep tattoo of
the hula girl, which he got in the Marines as a kid but was
still proud of, and how the Judge had never married because
he was so cantankerous no woman would have him — and
then the dogs. Pit bulls, dozens of them, locked in pens
and chained all over the yard of the Judge's ranch house.
There were photos too, of the dogs standing bandylegged
and grinning the way they do, like they're waiting for anybody to make a move, and the Judge scratching his favor-
ite one behind the ears, and throwing some slop to the
others.

Of course for the record the Judge said he didn't believe in
fighting his dogs, not for gambling or sport, because that was
against the law he had sworn to uphold. Besides, the Judge
felt it wasn't exactly humane to let dogs tear each other up
that way. "It might make a good show," the Judge had said,

lipping a cigarillo, "but I don't have the heart for it. I love 'em too much." The reporter had let him get away with that one. It was obvious to any thinking person that the Judge fought his dogs, because nobody had so many pit bulls for any other reason. That was what the breed was all about. Sure, they had laws against it, but nobody put a lot of effort into stopping it, and everybody knew it went on. It's a big sport in Arizona: Put two dogs in a ring and let them go at it until one is nothing but meat.

The fact that the Judge had a pack of ugly, vicious dogs, and the implication that he might be getting away with a little something by fighting them, only endeared him all the more to the voters, who had been returning him to the bench every four years, and probably would have kept him there if the Judge hadn't decided six terms was enough. That's the system we have in Arizona: By voting on whether or not to retain them we get judges no better than politicians. Leo Aloysius Harker was just the type we want in charge, a hard-ass, crusty and loud, tough on any criminals he didn't happen to agree with. Oh yeah, the Judge liked to dish out the punishment. He liked to deliver his lectures too, in the courtroom and now at every breakfast club and crimestopper banquet and to any reporter who needed a rush quote summing up the philosophy of right and wrong and evil that had to be stamped out before Friday. One of those judges that seem very much in style today, pinching every ass around the courthouse and never crossing his legs and coming in with a hangover to sentence drug users to the max while relishing the contradiction, the kind you expect to be wearing a Magnum and getting a blow from some pretty and impressionably ambitious law clerk under his robes during a trial — and even in retirement, at the annual Fourth of July softball game, high-spiking the public defenders. He was a real institution, wrapping himself in the red, white and blue and then pulling strings to get out of a parking ticket.

Which was why it was going to give me great pleasure to nail him. They might be winking about his fighting dogs now, they might be looking the other way, but once I had them paging through the blood in the breakfast edition, once I smeared them with the gore of his little hobby, they'd turn on him all right. He was an admired figure of unquestionable authority, the kind everybody deep down wants exposed as a despicable beast.

One thing bothered me more than the rest of it. The Judge was reaching back decades to get it on with Alice Malone. He was trying to prove something to himself, and that made him doubly dangerous. I was seeing those hot red smears on her belly again, burns from his fancy cigarillos. I was seeing him do it.

5

THE FIRST DOGFIGHT was the next night. I ran a couple of miles in the hottest part of the afternoon to empty myself out, and then put on old clothes I hoped would be camouflage. I had an hour to get nervous all over again, so I drove down to the river as the sun was calling it quits. Of course there wasn't any water there, this was an Arizona river, just a dry sandy bed crisscrossed by tire tracks. But down along the banks the bats were coming out of their hideouts to begin their nightly hunt. That's the kind of attraction we have here: furry little winged rats swooping and fluttering and scarfing down bugs. Actually I liked to watch them. After a few summers in the desert I started seeing them as graceful, overgrown butterflies. And I liked them for being primitive. Whenever I get to thinking these are civilized times I go out to watch the bats. That puts it all into perspective.

I leaned on my car and watched the first bats of evening winging by. I could see myself, there by the river. It would have made a good photo. You can't help thinking like that in the news business. Some fool bird was singing somewhere.

When it was dark I drove back to Alice Malone's trailer. She had hidden her legs inside faded jeans, and dressed like

an Arizona princess in a cowboy shirt with snaps up the front
and shit-kicker boots. The jeans were tight. So was she.

"Just keep your mouth shut and stick close to me. Don't
get creative." She inspected me. "Come here." She yanked
open my shirt from the neck down, popping off half the
buttons. "There. Now roll up your sleeves like a good ol'
boy."

We took her pickup because they would know it. Would
they ever. The hood had been stripped off, so the engine was
exposed, roaring and rocking, just about in our laps. Alice
stomped the clutch and gunned through the gears.

"You all right?"

"Just worry about yourself."

We went out in the country to the south. There was a thin
slice of moon. Alice had her hair tied back and it made her
look even fiercer. She didn't so much as glance at me for
twenty miles, or say much of anything. We got on some back
roads that cut off to the west, over a jumble of rocks that
qualifies as a mountain range in Arizona. There were plenty
of bumps that she didn't slow down for, and curves that gave
her a chance to throw me around the cab. The next valley was
only a couple of ranches, pinpricks of light miles apart. We
wound down into it and swung off on a rougher track through
some mesquites and over a hill and down to where they were
having it.

A couple dozen cars and pickups, the beds made over
with wire pens for hauling dogs, were parked any which
way around an old barn that was trying to lean all the way
over. Two guys with flashlights waved us down. One had a
shotgun. The other leaned in the window and shined in his
light.

"Hello, Alice."

"Get that light out of my face."

He aimed it down her shirt and into her lap and did a little pattern there. Alice fooled with the gas pedal, revving and letting off, revving and letting off. The light found me.

"Who's your friend?"

"My hairdresser, what d'you think?"

He laughed and waved us on in. We bounced over ruts and parked where we might not get bashed.

"Don't screw this up," she said.

She clamped onto my arm and we walked to the barn door. A guy straddling a hay bale just inside bored his eyes into us. He nodded and we went in. All the commotion was down at the other end in a smoky yellow haze. Under some hanging lights they had a ring, built out of bales and scrap lumber. Packed around it on slapped-together stands were guys yelling and waving cash; in the center, two dogs, pit bulls, were ripping at each other. Maybe you've heard about how these pit bulls will scarf down a poodle or tear into a grandmother or a kid like nothing, maybe you've even seen it happen. Well, that's just a little light amusement compared to what one of them will do to another of its breed. They make a whirlwind of snapping teeth and don't stop until one gets a crippling bite on the other. Once that happens, you could take a week off and come back and they'd still be fastened together like that, until the hurt one bleeds to death, or both of them starve. A pit bull will never let go of another pit bull on his own, not ever — they see it out to the end, and that's why they are so admired.

The fight we walked in on, one dog had its fangs buried in the chest of the other. They would thrash and growl a little and lie still, wheezing. Then they'd thrash again. They didn't make much noise or waste any motion. We got near enough to see the blood slicking down their fur, soaking into the dirt and straw, making their drool pink, and their eyes, wild and mad, and the holes in their hides, like they'd been stuck with forks. We were coming in late.

Alice said something I couldn't hear over the yelling. With a grip that was cutting off my circulation, she steered me into the crowd, elbowing to make a path. Some of them had to be ranchers, not the new style we have in Arizona, the dentists and stockbrokers who order a thousand acres by phone to impress themselves and set up a tax dodge, but the old style, out in the sun and the wind long enough that their faces looked no friendlier than any patch of desert. Some you could only call rednecks, with their swaggering beer guts and surly expressions and the duckbill caps that swore their allegiance to a team or corporation. There were also some women who looked like they belonged. Here and there, a pistol in a hip holster, or jammed under a belt. Nobody paid any special attention to Alice and me. They were watching the fight.

The Judge had stationed himself on the other side of the ring, where some of the handlers were waiting with their dogs. I'd seen his photos in the paper, I'd even been in his courtroom gallery a few times, and he wasn't hard to pick out. He had the dramatic looks that are all anyone really needs to get a following in Arizona: rawboned and rugged, with silver hair parted on the side and brushed back, shaggy eyebrows and a stirrup chin, and deep creases across his forehead and down his cheeks, so he never looked anything but stern. Perched behind the bench he was a towering figure, but of course in person he was short, five-five or five-six, and angry about it. I didn't see how he could recognize me — the kind of work I do, I don't let my face get around. But he was staring right at us.

A lot of what you do in journalism is bluff. Say you go out to shoot a riot and the people smashing things up or the cops smashing heads don't want their pictures in the paper, and so maybe they're thinking about smashing you and your camera — all you can do is aim your lens at them and make like you're backed by this powerful institution and the public's right to know all the bad news, when really all that's on the line at the moment is just you with that little 35 mm. Or as a reporter, say you suspect a guy of something — you get a little on him but not enough to nail him, so finally you face off with him in an interview and he doesn't know how much you have, for all he knows you've found out everything back to how he fucked over his best friend in the fifth grade. You play him a little bit and pretty soon he's nervous and spilling more than he wants to, and he winds up nailing himself. Those are a couple of ways bluffing comes into it, and there are plenty of others. After a while it gets to be a habit, and not only against sources. You might bluff the editors a little to make them think you're really onto something, when all you want is a couple of days out of the newsroom. You might even bluff the readers and make them think a story means more than it does. It's done all the time. Going up against all these dogfighters and the Judge, I had a lot of valuable journalistic experience.

Alice tugged me over to him. She coiled around me, warming me up. She had her own act going, and the Judge didn't go for it. She patted me on the chest, used my made-up name.

"This is Roy. Roy, meet the Judge."

I formed a smile, "Howdy," and stuck out my hand. It hung there.

"Where'd you find him?" the Judge boomed. His eyebrows needed combing. His eyes were flat brown, like old Mexican pesos.

"Roy's interested in the dogs."

"And what else? He's here, isn't he? We have some fine specimens in the ring tonight."

"Pretty good," I said.

He stared at me. Alice hugged me, slid her hand around back inside my belt. "You fighting Devil?"

The Judge nodded once. "Not that there's any competition."

Squealing broke out in the ring and the Judge turned to look. Two handlers had gone in to pry the dogs apart and haul them into opposite corners. One dog was in trouble. Its rear legs weren't working. The handler grabbed it behind the neck and twisted, coaching it, aiming it back into the ring. In the far corner the other handler was doing the same with his dog. That's how they run these fights — they can't wait around for the dogs to settle it, they have to speed things up.

The pit bulls grinned wickedly, panting, glaring at each other with red eyes. They weren't big dogs, pit bulls never are, but they were monsters, all chest and jaws.

"They've been going an hour and a half now," the Judge said.

The referee, a shirtless fat man bulging out of a red vest, dropped his hand, and the dogs were loosed. The lame one dragged itself forward, trying to attack. The other circled briefly for an opening and struck. They whipped around, hitting teeth. Alice dug her fingers into me. The handlers went in and crouched down, screaming:

"Rip him, rip him."

"Get up, Pancho, get up now."

The crowd screamed for a kill. We had our own little hell going there under the dirty yellow light. The Judge pulled out one of his cigarillos and went through the routine of firing it up. He puffed clouds of smoke into the haze.

"Come on, you bastard Pancho."

"Don't let him up, boy, don't let him up."

The ref signaled and they pried the dogs apart. The handlers had blood smeared to their elbows. The lame dog bubbled pink froth from its lips and the holes in its chest. It struggled to stand on its front paws.

"He's game, he's game."

"It ain't over yet."

"Let 'em go, let 'em go."

"Finish it."

The ref huddled with the handlers. He shrugged, and they got the dogs ready again. The lame one went down silently in the other's jaws. That was it.

The Judge tapped a long ash off his cigarillo. "No surprises."

They were carrying the dogs out, and they were doing it tenderly. The loser looked dead, but his eyes were open and blinking. A woman laughed. The crowd had subsided to a loud murmur. All around us they were passing cash, settling the bets. The Judge looked at Alice and me.

"No surprises," he repeated. He walked off.

I pushed Alice away. "Point it somewhere else."

"Why? You don't like it?" She hugged me again, rubbing her chest across my arm. She was good at it, and I let her — to avoid making a scene, and just to let her.

"He doesn't like it."

"He's that way with everyone."

"Whatever is between you and him, you work it out. I'm here for my own purpose."

"You're here because I brought you."

"So you can make him squirm."

"He needs it. Don't disappoint me."

I was tempted to do just that. But after what I'd seen, in

the dog ring and the faces around it, there was no way I was going to. I had ahold of a story, one I wanted bad, and I wasn't about to let it go. I was going to nail every son of a bitch that was there, and she was going to help me do it.

"Just ease off," I told her. "We're after the same thing."

She dug into her jeans for the keys to her pickup, and stuffed them into my pants pocket.

"Anytime it gets to be too much for you, don't hesitate."

She was playing me again, and she was good at it.

The Judge fought his dog next. They had a little ceremony, a weigh-in, before it started, on a scale that had no pan, just a hook, made for slinging bales of cotton. When the Judge came out with his dog, which was black, and wagging its tail, the crowd let out a ragged cheer.

"Devil!"

"Go Devil!"

The Judge lifted Devil and hung him on the scale, collar over the hook. Devil dangled there while the ref took a reading.

"Fifty-eight, six."

The Judge unhooked Devil and let him down. Devil wagged his tail some more. Another handler went through the same routine with his dog, a brown one named Bummer.

"Fifty-nine, two."

"Won't do him any good." That got a round of laughs.

The Judge led Devil into the ring, and the other handler followed with Bummer. The dogs wagged away. They were pointed into their corners. It was peaceful as long as they couldn't see each other. Around the ring the bets were coming down, the line two-to-one against Bummer. Then the dogs were turned. That quickly, they lunged, rushing in a blur, and even over the yells you could hear them smack together. They rumbled around trying to have each other for supper, and in no time Bummer was down — Devil had a jaw-lock on his throat. They rested in that position while the crowd goaded them on. It wasn't a killing hold. Now and then Devil would shake Bummer and worry him a little.

"How long will this take?"

Alice stared at the dogs. "That Devil."

"How long?"

She blew out her lungs. "A while. They have to get their money's worth."

"I'll be back."

But she tagged right along.

I had been looking the place over, and it seemed like I might be able to climb a section of the stands, get the right angle, and snap some photos of the fight without anyone noticing. I knew it was risky, but I wanted to show the Judge with his dog in action. I wanted photos that, even at a glance, would have him indisputably nailed.

The stands were planks only three rows high, but we got some altitude climbing up to the top row. There was no one next to us. Most of them were closer to the ring, and lower down. As we watched the fight, I tried to spot anyone watching us. They were aiming the dogs for another charge. After a mad brawl Devil wound up on top again, Bummer's blood smeared on his muzzle. Bummer writhed around under him. Looking down on the ring, the lights showing every muscle in the dogs, with the crowd surging around them, would have made a photo you'd never get over. It would have hit you like a kick in the nuts.

We seemed to be in the clear.

Not being obvious about it, I went for my camera, one of these new wafer models smaller than a cigarette pack. I had it strapped to my calf with Velcro. With the film I had loaded

in it, I didn't need a flash; I couldn't have gotten away with
that, even with all the ruckus. I didn't need to do any
focusing with the lens. My problem was aiming. I palmed
the camera and held it down between my knees, and shot
from there, changing my frame a little each time. It had been
hot all along — this was an Arizona night, stoked up by the
crowd and the smoke — but I hadn't noticed myself sweating until I started to take pictures.

Alice saw what I was trying to do and moved down in front
of me, not in line with my shots, but just to the left, so she
blocked anybody's view from that angle. The Judge was right
where I wanted him, crouched over Devil in the ring. Just as I
ran off some shots, two rednecks on the other side of Alice
leaped up suddenly, shoving and cuffing. One toppled
my way and would have dropped in my lap if Alice hadn't
braced him.

"Take it for a walk," she said.

He got himself upright and shoved the other one. Clowns.
Down below the dogfight was ending. There wasn't a part of
Bummer that hadn't been chewed. Devil was declared the
winner. No surprises. I ran out the roll and Alice nestled back
between my legs while I Velcroed the camera away.

"Get what you wanted?"

"For now."

"Nice company I've been keeping, eh?"

"Just your average citizens of Arizona."

"You got that right."

We sat there like any couple. She shifted around and made
a little man with her fingers and walked him up over my
knee.

"Newspaperman, what's he up to now?"

She walked her fingers up my thigh, and across, and down
to my other knee.

"Newspaperman, what's he digging into?"

My blood was up. It was the wrong time for her fingers, which made it the right time — anything is better when it's dangerous, or you might as well stay home with the remote control.

"Don't try to pretend with me," she said. "You get off on this, that's why you do it. You shouldn't, so you do. You get off on me, right here, right now."

Down below they were getting set for another fight. I brushed off her little man but she had him right back on the job.

"Let's go," I told her. "I've seen enough."

"Have you."

She climbed over me using creative handholds and jumped down behind the stands. I had to go after her. There were some bales stacked up for supports, and she backed me up against one.

"They have a rule. Nobody leaves until the last fight is over."

She giggled and leaned against me. All night she'd been on me. She had to stop or else. I palmed her through the cowboy shirt, and squeezed. She grabbed me where she shouldn't have and squeezed back. Everybody had been getting away with things, and now beyond smart or stupid it was my turn to dabble just a bit. I was Roy for the night and I yanked on her ponytail and she sank her teeth into my neck. There were yells from the ring and two more dogs smacked together. The fight got louder. She stabbed her hand into my pants, curling her fingers into my hairs and tugging, stinging me as she hooked her other arm around my ears and bit my chin, then she lifted her legs and fastened herself against me. I had to stumble down on one knee and forced her to ride the other one until she squirmed, and when she got too good at

that, I flopped us over on her back, whooshing the air out of
her lungs, trying to plug her mouth with my tongue. As she
struggled for breath I ripped her shirt down off her shoulders
and dug my thumbs into her collarbones and she arched
under me. The dogs went at it and so did we.

6

O F COURSE we had to be interrupted. Grabbed by the neck, I got hauled off her and out from under the stands, thrown down, choked and dragged. They had a noose around my neck on one end of a pole, the rig they use on unruly dogs. Working the other end was a big lug, and there was another one holding Alice. And the Judge. I couldn't reach any of them or anything but the pole, and that did me no good at all. They kept me down and kept on with that noose, then eased up just a little so I could breathe. The Judge fired up a cigarillo.

"You could have waited until you got outside. You could have gone out in the goddamn bushes."

I got my fingers in under the noose to save my neck, and stood up. They let me. The lug holding the pole had sick eyes, clouded white. His compadre was skinny-mean with lemon hair down his back. Several others were hanging back aways, watching to see how it came out. The Judge blew a cloud of smoke at Alice.

"I don't really care what you do. But don't do it right in my face. Don't do it just to spoil my evening."

"What's the matter?" she said. "Afraid you'll stain your pants?" The Judge flushed. "Shorty's excitable."

He hopped over and slapped her twice. "You want a little exhibition? You want it right now?"

I strained out, "Get this thing off me."

"You," the Judge pointed his cigarillo at me, "don't give anyone advice." He waved his arm. "Bring them around."

They yanked me with the pole, around front of the stands, shoving Alice along, into the dog ring under the dirty yellow lights. The dogs had been taken out. The crowd closed around us.

"Before you go home," the Judge boomed out, "we have one more match. You could call it the finale, but frankly I just don't know if it'll amount to anything. A moment ago I caught these two groping each other behind the stands."

There was a round of snickers.

"I thought they might like to finish it out here."

That got him whistles and yells.

"Yeah. Yeah."

"Whooooeeee."

"Show. Show. Show. Show."

He held up a fan of twenties. "I'll take any bets, I don't think they have the gumption."

There we were in the center of a riot. They slipped the noose off me, and the Judge and the other two backed away, leaving Alice and me alone to face it.

"Rip her, rip her."

"Take him down."

"Eat him up."

"Show. Show. Show. Show."

When I walked to the edge of the ring, two or three of them shoved me back. Alice latched onto me. They were throwing whatever they had — a cup of beer splashed over us. Alice picked it up and crumpled it and flung it back at them. A lit cigarette tapped off my cheek, fluffing sparks.

Something slapped my arm, twisted down into the dirt — a
dog collar and leash. Crushed ice hailed on us. The faces and
mouths made a wall, the yells mixing and solidifying, pressing from all sides, thick in my throat as I tried to breathe
them in. I wanted to cover my eyes and ears and fold into a
ball. Alice snatched up the leash and ran at the faces and
started whipping. Some of them grabbed the leash and
reached down and grabbed her, ripping her shirt some more.
My thoughts had to shout: Get over there and beat them off
her, Macky, and don't let that little sock on the ear discourage
you. Beat on the arm that has the nice scar and the one with
the Navajo wristband and the one that's missing a finger.
Knock her loose! Her eyes popping — foam on her lips —
and she's tearing the shirt all the way off, pitching down the
rag. Don't touch her, it's what they want! Her breasts glowing
in the yellow light, her nipples gone soft — she can paralyze
the moment, intimidate the yelling, cow them into silence.
Stare as she straightens up and drops her arms with that look
of understanding. Take a stunner on the head — some cretin
lobbed a shoe. Stand up against the yells that are surging
again as she pivots and taunts them madly with her breasts —
"Is this it? Is this it?" — no matter how much they want her,
she's making it a real Fuck You! Here comes the other shoe,
duck. Now a new her — lips quivering and chest heaving,
she won't be the least bit predictable, despite all of it doesn't
she look elegant!

Trembling, she hugged me, my arms went around her, as
everyone screamed us on.

We stood there together at the bottom of the world as they
pelted us with apple cores and wadded dollar bills and con-
dom packets. My every muscle and nerve and square inch of
skin were tensed, my senses blasting. I could take the crowd

and every version of her. In my arms now she was as tender as any narcotic — already with her wild swings she was reaching too deeply into me, too close to who I really was. Before it had been an act for both of us; the roaring reality of the ring was forcing us to own up. She started small, closing her eyes and hiding her face in my neck, her flanks pillowed inside my palms, the gulley of her spine drawing my fingertips. Gradually the yelling and the faces receded until they were somewhere way out there in the distance and she was the larger risk. I got hard against her, and she pressed her waist-up softness closer. Her trembling gave way to an eerie vibration I could feel emanating from her chest and throat: She was humming, steadying herself and powering us. The yellow lights began to flash off and on, off and on. The strobing brought me up out of her and I heard the yelling loud again, but as distinct and fewer voices. No Judge. I held Alice and she hummed into me as they drifted past and out the door, dropping coins and insults: "Whore." "Prick." "Cop-outs." — the yellow lights strobing on all of us. Then the lights flashed off for good and somebody in silhouette at the door called out in a singsong, "*Buenas noches.*" It was just Alice and me in the darkness. She pushed off me without a word. As we caught our breath, I became acutely aware of the space between us. In the faint moonlight leaking through the slats of the barn she was a shadow, panting.

"You're a real buckeroo, aren't you?" she said harshly.

Ahead of me again. "Even the women are, around here."

"You like being the main attraction?"

I had a couple of answers to that, about how she'd started it, but she'd slipped the dirk in just right, and now she was trembling, seeming fragile again. She had me off balance and amazed, so I could only ask, "How many of you are there?"

"You got your pictures?" She took long strides to the door, crashed it open, vanished.

I forced myself to check the little camera that was still strapped to my leg: It seemed to be intact. Then I ran after her, to her pickup, starkly isolated on the rutted field.

She was fuming in the driver's seat, still topless and smooth about it. "Keys," she ordered. She took them out of my hand and barely let me climb into the passenger's side as she fired up the truck and spun out. We sat apart, not touching, just looking out the windshield at the skeleton of the engine rocking on its mounts. Somebody had drawn a heart in lipstick on the windshield. I wanted to say something to her, something manly and incisive to shore us up, but I didn't know what the hell to think of any of it myself. We chased the moon back to Tucson — from low on the horizon it smirked at both of us. When we got to her place she slammed out of the pickup and into the trailer. I followed her in, watched her hunt up a little fold of cocaine and snort doses off her fingertips. She took the coke into the bedroom and marched out with an armload of clothes, loose and on hangers, that she dropped in a pile in the front yard. She marched out with another load and dumped it on the first. Then the sheets and the bedspread. She snatched up towels, pillows, lamps, the radio, the TV. I sat on the front step and stayed out of her way — anything else I might try was going to be wrong. She stripped the trailer and piled everything in the yard and snatched a can of gas out of the pickup. When I tried to block her she grunted and barged past me and sloshed gas over the pile and lit it all on fire. It went with a *whoosh*. She tugged off her boots and hurled one and then the other into the flames. The TV picture tube popped. She stripped off her jeans and hurled them in. The panties followed. Flames licked into the black sky, lit up her body, and reflected in her eyes. She crouched and pulled out a flaming towel and started for the trailer. That's when I knocked her down.

"Alice Malone. Do you hear me? That's enough."

She hissed and flung herself against me, beating me and scratching. I had to get us out of there before somebody came looking for the fire. I wrestled her over to my car and shoved her in. She didn't want my hands on her. She tried to leap out and when I stopped her, she curled herself against the passenger door. I got a blanket out of the trunk and covered her with it and drove us out of there, into the city where women in her condition were less noticeable, to the only place I could think to take her.

I was having a guest after all. She still hadn't cried.

I gave her a downer with a glass of tequila and put her to bed. In the dark she lay rigidly on her side under the sheet, staring at the wall where the streetlamp coming through the blinds left a pattern of bars. I sat in a chair with my feet propped on the bed beside her, drinking tequila and smoking an old pack of cigarettes, studying how the red glow consumed the paper and stale tobacco. I had the camera on the table and the roll of film from the dogfight. It was going to be a hell of a story, if I could still pull it off. My neck was sore from the noose and I had nicks and scratches, and maybe it was my share. I thought about that and about all the ifs and maybes. Alice Malone didn't sleep and she didn't move or look at me. She was my Arizona date.

7

I CAN TELL YOU what it's like to work for a newspaper. Imagine a combine, one of those huge threshing machines that eat up a row of wheat like nothing, bearing right down on you. You're running in front of it, all day long, day in, day out, just inches in front of the maw, where steel blades are whirring and clacking and waiting for you to get tired or make one slip. The only way to keep the combine off you is to throw it something else to rip apart and digest. What you feed it is stories. Words and photos. Ten inches on this, fifteen inches on that, a vertical shot here and a horizontal there, scraps of news and film that go into the maw where they are processed and dumped out on some page to fill the spaces around the ads. Each story buys you a little time, barely enough to slap together the next story, and the next, and the next. You never get far ahead, you never take a breather, all you do is live on the hustle. Always in a rush, always on deadline, you keep scrambling to feed the combine. That's what it's like. The only way to break free is with a big story, one you can ride for a while and tear off in pieces so big, the combine has to strain to choke them down. That buys you a little time. But sooner or later the combine will come chomping after you again, and you better be ready to feed it all over again.

So when these editors and their lackeys and the academic types start sniffing about ethics and principles and holding up this business as a profession, all I can do is laugh. The object is to get the story, any way you can. The only principle is don't be wrong with a fact, because then the combine will take your arm off, or worse. You might get sucked in and come out the other end a night copy editor, or the guy who handles the box scores over in sports. You could spend the rest of your career loading film rolls for the real shooters. You could end up unemployed, or whacked by a lawsuit over one lousy fact. That's what the combine can do to you. So you keep feeding it and hustling with an eye out for the big story and hope you don't make a mistake. How you get any story, that's irrelevant. You think the public cares? They just want the goods on whoever you're nailing, that's all. But it's hard to do a proper job on someone with the combine breathing down your neck.

So the papers are full of fluff that's easy to pick up on the run, speeches and crashes and any bad weather that happens to occur anywhere on the planet, and fascinating profiles of the button collector next door, any fluff as long as you can get it quick and the combine can shred it up to fit neatly around the ads. The real stories, the ones everybody knows are out there, the tough stories about how things really work and who is behind it, they don't make it into the news. Damn few reporters go around nailing anyone anymore and it's a shame, because there are plenty out there who need it done to them. But there's just no time when you're only a half-step ahead of the machine.

Sitting there in the dark with Alice Malone, I could feel the combine's blades whispering close behind me, and I could tell myself to do whatever was necessary to get this story. That's why I'd grabbed her behind the stands, and that's why I brought her home. Yeah, that's the reason — for the story. She'd wanted me to grab her and I had to play it her way, didn't I? If I hadn't, who knows what she would have done? She could've blown my cover and the photos and any possibility of a story. It's got nothing to do with how she feels under my hands. Nothing to do with how she looks naked by firelight. Nothing to do with the sheer pleasure of breaking every little rule and for once letting loose. Nothing at all. The story was going to be harder to get now, with the two of us thrust in the dog ring together, where she'd surprised me with her tenderness and vulnerability even as she was showing more steel than any woman I'd ever known. If she tripped me up now, we'd both go down. She might just torch my place if I gave her a chance. That would be a story. But not one I wanted to be part of . . .

Long about dawn she wrapped herself in the sheet and came out on the porch, where I was trying to take comfort in any stray bats that might be fluttering by. Dawn is the other rush hour for them. All the bats had been out hunting since sunset, gulping insects by the city lights, and now they were flying back to their hidey-holes. One did a dance in the air for us.

She tried her voice, ragged. "The way it flies, it's beautiful."

"There aren't many people who'd think so."

The bat fluttered off to some dark roost. Alice coughed and adjusted the sheet. "I'm groggy, Macky. What did you give me?"

"A sleeping pill."

"I didn't sleep."

"I didn't either."

"I can still hear the screaming — they really wanted us to

do it right in front of them. All night I could hear them. What did they have against us?"

"I don't know. The usual."

"Next time I might just do it. Think they'd shut up then? The way their faces looked. He worked them into it. He led them on. I was through with him before we went out there."

"Whatever you say."

"I couldn't stand anything that reminded me of him. I couldn't live in that trailer. I couldn't keep anything he'd bought me. I had to burn it all."

"It was fine with me. I've thought about it myself. Pile up everything I own and burn it and dance around naked. Someday I'll get it done."

"Go to hell."

"I mean it."

She padded back inside the house. After a while I heard the shower running. She'd surprised me again with how alert she was to every nuance. I'd been up all night drawing dimensions around her and in a blink she had broken out again. My business was being certain about how people and things worked and I was damn tired of it, and she seemed to sense that too. She was keeping me interested with her surprises, and with how she cocked her chin down to emphasize her eyes and deepened her voice and slowed the world to the speed of her coaxing and made you think she knew things she couldn't have.

The sun was too hot on the porch — another Arizona morning getting worse by the minute. I went in and shut the door to block it out and switched on the cooler. I started another cigarette and ground it out and crushed the pack and threw it away. That was something accomplished. The shower fell silent. She came out of the bathroom in my red flannel robe — her hair wet, the flannel damp and clinging. That routine.

"Before you burn your own stuff, I need something to wear."

I got out one of my T-shirts and a pair of hiking shorts and flopped them on the bed. She didn't show the slightest interest.

"I know what's bothering you. It's your story. I've put a glitch in it, haven't I?" She fingered her hair, separating the wet strands. "That's all that matters to you, isn't it?"

"And not to you? You called me up. You wanted a guy nailed."

"And I'll make sure he is. If it isn't with a newspaper story, it'll be some way else. There are plenty of ways to nail a man."

"You know about that?"

"Somebody has to be blamed — so make it me. I lured you down to that dogfight, I came on to you, I got you into that ring. That's how it was?"

I should've listened closer. But by then, of course, I was studying how the robe fit her. As much of her as I'd seen the night before, it had been without intimacy like this, and now she had me thinking that inside the robe were more of her surprises. I was gliding on her dusky skin, down her neck, up her legs, thinking there was no harm in gliding, that I could stop anytime and not get in any deeper.

"It wasn't just me," she said.

"I know," I told her. "The screaming — I can hear it too. I know how to shut them up. Last night was just the opener. I want to take in more of these dogfights. And I'm not done with the Judge. His ranch — he trains dogs for the ring out there, doesn't he? You get me in."

"Oh sure."

"He won't have any hard feelings, not against you, not if you don't want him to. If he does, I'll be there."

"You were there last night. He had you in a noose."

"That was just humiliation. You can handle him."

She fooled with the ends of the sash, the once-over twist that held the robe closed. "I'll help you, and it doesn't have anything to do with you."

"I know that."

"Good. Just keep it in mind."

I laughed. "Next you'll want to move in."

"I thought I had. I could sleep on the couch."

"I don't think so."

"Just you and all this dead cactus. You couldn't handle me?"

"My editor couldn't."

"He wouldn't find out."

"He finds out everything."

"Not everything, Macky."

"Almost. You can't stay here. The Judge'll want to know where you've landed, he might get the notion to pay you a visit, and I can't have him talking to the landlord or the neighbors or getting the idea to run the license plate on my car. Once he finds out my real name, and links me to the paper, the story stops there. You have any money? Know anyone else in town? Somebody who'd take you in?"

"Sure I do. The Judge has a lot of friends."

"No one else? Where do you come from, anyway?"

"Now you want my résumé? Nevada."

"Where in Nevada?"

"Laughlin." She shrugged. "I worked in the casinos, where everybody goes to strike it rich. That's why I'm broke. What about you paying me? Is that out now?"

"I'll get the paper to put you up at a motel."

"What about what I want? I don't like motels. Even when they're full, they're empty."

"Well, that's what we're offering."

"Okay, Macky. If that's it."

"That's it." If I said it enough times, I might believe it.

8

I STASHED HER at the Paradise Motel — two-story cellblocks around a concrete patio and a teardrop pool, four or five disheveled palm trees, under the noise of the interstate.

"It's been a while since you guys won a Pulitzer, hasn't it?" she said.

She was barefoot and lost inside my shorts and T-shirt. I gave her cash for the room and a meal. "Keep the receipts. The business office is pretty sticky."

"Too sticky to spring for shoes?"

"I'll ask."

"You aren't getting rid of me, are you?"

"Just for a couple of hours."

I drove down to the paper to run the film from the dogfight. The prints looked strong. Some of them were framed cockeyed and half the time the dogs were blurred but that just added to the feeling of sudden brute violence. There were some real Arizona postcards.

I took a folder of them to Rissler's office. "Macky. I didn't see you come in. What've we got? These are hard to look at, aren't they? Talk about raw. Jesus, what that black one is doing to the other one. It's a slaughter. Even a dog deserves better. That's the Judge? Gentlemanly fellow, isn't he. Oh yeah. He loves his little Blackie, doesn't he. Nice little Blackie. Give him a biscuit."

"Devil. That's the dog's name."

"Come off it."

"No. Devil."

"Well, it's descriptive. No use calling any of these things Lassie, or Spot. How many do you have? Is this it?"

"That little camera won't take a bigger load."

"Couldn't change rolls? That wouldn't be feasible, would it, not in this crowd. Wouldn't want them on your case. This guy's got teeth like the dogs. Where'd they have this, some barn?" I told him what he needed to know. "How about this Alice Malone? She cooperating?"

"You could say that. She's not exactly steady. She kind of freaked out after the dogfight."

"What do you mean?"

"She made a fire, burned some stuff. Everything."

"Everything?"

"She broke with the Judge. He'd paid the tab for all of it."

"So she cleaned out her closets. Couldn't she have waited until we had the story? What else? I see those scratches. Your neck's scraped too. Somebody try to strangle you?"

"There was a little problem. It didn't amount to much."

"Macky. Was it her?"

"You could say that."

"Just another source trying to choke you, that it, Macky? All in a night's work? You make journalism so exciting. Should I ask why she did it?"

"I told you. She freaked out."

"And came after the media. Isn't that how it always happens? You can't tell it straight, can you? Never mind. As long as she's cooperating. She better keep her hands off you until we get this story. Or I'll strangle the both of you. You get me? Does this mean we've lost access to the Judge?"

"I'm hoping he'll give her another chance, or at least not drive her off."

"She going to last through this?"

"What about me?"

"All right. I'll keep these." He slid the prints in a drawer and locked it. "Just in case something more serious happens to you."

Of course he was already appropriating the story. My story. "It's nice you're so concerned. If I do wind up in some dumpster, it'd make a better story — that'd give you some consolation."

"A bit." He held out his hand, and I had to give him five. "I never know when you're kidding, Macky. What's left to get?"

"I'll try to shoot the Judge training his dogs, and at some more fights, so it's clear he wasn't just passing through. I want more crowd shots, so we can ID as many others as we can. I need your okay on expenses."

"What for? Some new gizmo for the camera?"

"I put her up in a motel. She's got no place to land and she needs money for food and clothes."

"So she's on our tab now. If these prints weren't as good as they are, I'd tell you no. Just keep it down. And now that we're paying, try to keep her away from matches, will you? If we can pull this off, it'll go national. It's got all the elements. This could mean a Pulitzer."

"She was just mentioning that this morning."

"I'll worry about the Pulitzer. You two just work the story, and make it good. And don't take too long either."

*   *   *

She was starving so I took her to lunch at one of those hallowed franchise joints they have on every other corner, all with the same menu and the orange plastic booths and the food tasting like it had been trucked in from a central warehouse.

"You've got some taste in restaurants. The same taste you've got in motels."

"We're not on vacation."

"I can tell."

They didn't want to let her in barefoot and that cost me an extra dollar. That's all you have to pay in Arizona to put your feet into someone else's soup. She ordered half the menu and I had eggs and a plastic pot of coffee. The last night was catching up to me, and she wasn't helping.

"The paper says it might not be so hot today. Says it might not break a hundred."

"Then it'll hit one-oh-five for sure."

"How long you been hustling for that rag?"

"Seven years."

"And before that?"

"I was on a smaller paper in Colorado."

"So you're moving up. Taking some time, isn't it?"

"There aren't that many big papers anymore or many openings. I'll be moving up pretty soon."

"Meanwhile here you are. Somehow I don't get the idea you care for Arizona too much."

"What makes you say that?"

She pointed her fork at me. "You're confined, Macky. They pay you peanuts so you can rent that shitty doll house and drive that overheating Chevy. You call it even by sneaking around nailing people. You take it out on everyone."

"There's more to it than that."

"Sure. You're doing good. But why are you doing it?" She had done some sneaking up on her own and now she wanted an answer. I was fooling with the handle of my coffee mug. She shifted and touched my hand with the pointed tines of her fork, applied pressure. "Right, wrong, one comes out of the other. You're an example. I don't think in words. I make it personal. You're not talking, Macky." She let up with the fork and I looked at the tracks the tines had left in my hand.

"I didn't know I was on the menu."

"Everybody is." She stroked the tracks with the curved underside of the fork. "What about women? You take it out on them too?"

"If they want me to."

"You seeing anyone?"

"Some. Two or three."

"None of them have any power, not if they let you divide your attention like that. What do you do with them? Take them to places like this, go home in the missionary position? Ever really get wild? I don't mean simulated wild, like when you're sneaking around on a story, but really wild?"

"I jump off a tall rock."

"What?"

I batted away the fork and swigged some plastic coffee. "A very tall rock. And I don't pop the chute until the last second."

"Oh, with a parachute. I heard about people who do that. Like off the Eiffel Tower, or that big cliff at Yosemite. You take any of these women to jump with you?"

"It's not a social thing."

"No, I guess not."

"Anyway, they don't get it."

"I do, Macky. I get it perfectly. You're confined on the top of that rock and then you jump" — she slapped the table, whisked her hand high, let it fall slowly, made a fist — "and it only lasts so long and then you're confined to that parachute and back where you started, Arizona. You do anything else wild? Anything without a parachute?"

"Like what? Wind up barefoot dressed in somebody else's clothes?"

"You try to sound so tough. Are you really tough, or just simulated tough?"

"My nose hasn't been broken yet."

She touched the bump on hers, and got melancholy. "I didn't get it fixed. I wanted to look a shade crooked."

"You do. How'd it happen?"

"A man did it."

"I knew that."

"He wasn't tough at all."

"Why is it you can ask me anything and tell me all about my life and I don't get to ask you the simplest questions?"

"You haven't told me anything. You want to investigate me? Go ahead. Ask away."

"What were you doing up in those Laughlin casinos?"

"You think I was tricking? Yeah, you do. Because I look pretty good to you, don't I, Macky? Let's leave you wondering about that. Let's say I was slinging drinks."

"How'd you fall in with the Judge?"

"The Judge. He'd come up every so often to gamble and fool around. Once he crossed the state line he'd go into his Mister Hyde. Lot of people do. He invited me down here."

"And you went for it."

"You ever been to Laughlin? It makes Vegas look like Monte Carlo."

"So it didn't matter who was asking you."

"It mattered. Whatever else the Judge is, he's not a sucker and he's not a wimp. He's not dull or squirrelly or drugged

out and he doesn't drive a BMW. He can be entertaining. I
liked his tattoo."

"Sounds like true love."

"Simulated, that's all. He's just another lonely man."

"And you?"

"Lonely? Is that where your investigation is leading?"

"What were you doing before Laughlin?"

"I went around in white dresses picking flowers and opening presents that young men brought me. Then I had an
overdue library book, and here I am." She puckered up and
fluttered her hand over her mouth to make a warpath cry,
"*Woo-woo-woo-woo-woo.*"

"Got some Indian blood in you?"

"Sure. My great-uncle was Sitting Bull himself."

"So you're a simulated Indian."

"That's all there are anymore."

We went round and round. She had talked about power
and women. She would know. She had me under siege just
sitting there and she could make any sentence intimate. Or
simulated intimate. It was obvious what the Judge, or any
man, saw in her. Yeah, Macky, No don't do it, Yeah, No —
that was the argument she ran inside me, a dangerous argument, and that's what she had on me, more than the sex
alone. I tried to not let her get to me like she had at the
dogfight. We drove to a discount store and she made it
difficult, picking out an outfit. I was settling the bill when
she stepped out of the changing room, and even the woman
clerk reacted to her. She was hanging out of a miniskirt and
one of those band tops that didn't cover her shoulders or those
three red smears — the cigarillo burns on her belly. Her feet
still looked bare in sandals that tied around her ankles. You'd
think with skin as dusky as hers she'd stick to colors but no,
the outfit, what there was of it, was black.

"Glad you got something nice and conservative."

"I dress for the heat, okay?"

But she was furious, another of her abrupt swings, and she let me have it in the parking lot. "You look at me, what do you see? You see *this*." She grabbed her tit. "You see *this*." And her ass. "You don't see Alice Malone. And neither will the Judge or those rednecks at the dogfight or anybody else. This is the best protection I could have. In this I'm just another squeeze."

She stomped around the car and slammed herself into it. I got behind the wheel. The sun had fired up the interior — of course there isn't a single parking lot in all the hundreds of thousands of paved acres in Arizona that has even a sliver of shade. The seat, the wheel, the door handles, everything was scalding. She jammed on the controls for the air-conditioning.

"Doesn't this work?"

"No."

"Why should it?" She propped her feet on the dash, bunching the skirt around her hips, and spread her legs.

"If you ride like that I'm going to have an accident."

"Think I'm a front-seat tease?" Slowly, exaggerating her movements, she lowered her legs. "That better?"

Some of what happened I can blame on Arizona. The awful heat made it harder for both of us to act the least bit civilized. I'd look at her on the seat next to me and see the beads of sweat collecting along her upper lip and glistening on her chest and belly and legs and I'd smell her sweating like the animal she was. Like we both were. The heat was building up in me and it was hard to think about anything but taking her, really taking her, and if I ever did it wasn't going to be any of this good-loving in the songs — it was going to

be bad-loving, and she knew it and wanted it, and the longer
we delayed the more bad and better it would be. There we
were. There's no more primitive place than the desert and we
were proving it. I tried to keep my eyes on the road and she
never asked where we were going. She just sat there licking
the sweat off her upper lip, fingering it off her cheekbones
and temples and the back of her neck. I tried to think about
the job we were supposed to be doing, and how to approach
it, and all I could come up with was: bluntly. We drove out to
her old place, the sagging trailer with the heap of ashes in the
yard, her charred clothes and charred junk and charred past
life. It didn't seem like anybody had been out to investigate
the fire — why should anybody bother? She'd left the keys in
the pickup, but nobody had gotten around to stealing it
either. She got the pickup going and trailed me back to my
place. I left my car there and took the tiniest camera I had,
made for real spying, and got in the truck. We pretended to
ignore every little thing about each other and the lipsticked
heart from our night at the dogfight that was melting now on
the windshield as we started out to visit the Judge.

9

THE RANCH HOUSE was one of those chic ones slopped together out of adobe mud and maintained for a couple hundred years with layers of more mud. It was back in a mesquite grove with a long gravel driveway winding in across a couple of dry washes and through a stringy bunch of cattle and a minefield of cowflops. There was a big porch across the front with pole timbers and a pole railing and a shorter pole hitching post, below which was a dappling of horseflops. That's the sort of subtle distinction you learn to make in Arizona, cowflop versus horseflop, it's a matter of shading and shape of the flop. A horde of flies was buzzing around and locusts rasped in the trees and somewhere a donkey was braying. We made it onto the porch without stepping in anything. There was a screen door and a man standing behind it.

"Hello, Ed."

"Alice. Thought that sounded like your truck. I was hoping it wasn't."

"Ed's eyes aren't too good. Come on out, Ed. Meet the man you were dog-poling last night."

He opened the screen and stepped out, six inches larger than me in every direction, with a massive unmoving face and those blank milky eyes. Cataracts, pretty far along. In one hand he had a thick book, closed around a thick finger. The title and markings were worn off. "You like to continue it?"

"No."

"Where is he?" Alice asked.

"He's in seclusion. In an ugly mood."

"I'll let him tell me that," Alice said. "You're not calling any shots around here."

"Better let him alone. He's been drunk since midnight. Sick about you and this character and what you've done. He's been thinking violent thoughts."

"Your eyes must be getting worse, Ed. We didn't do anything to upset anybody."

"My eyes. I can't read my Charlie Dickens. I turn the pages and recall what lines I can. But I don't need eyes to track you. I can smell you coming. Any trouble, Alice, you're right in the middle of it."

I told him, "You're taking us wrong. We don't want any trouble at all. We came out here to avoid it. To make peace." I blew some more of that at him. He got tired of listening. "The Judge's out back."

The Judge had made the swimming pool his throne. He was sitting in the far end, on the steps descending into the shallows, so the water lapped his waist. He had a straw cowboy hat down low over his eyes, a bottle of bourbon and some in a glass on ice within reach, and he was puffing on one of his thin black cigarillos. Under a surface tan, the skin on his chest and shoulders was sunburned red. Sitting next to him, half-immersed, was the black pit bull, Devil. Both of them studied our approach. I had the spy camera palmed and snapped a couple shots of them, paired up like that, and then pocketed the camera as we got closer.

"I'm busted," the Judge boomed out. "They got us, Devil. Under any number of statutes. The infamous crime against nature. The lewd or lascivious or unnatural act."

Alice asked, "What are you doing with him in there?"

"You're busted too. The both of you. Cohabitation. It's still on the books. They'll have to take us all in." He threw back his head and laughed soundlessly. "Everybody slips up somewhere. Ever disclose the content of a telephone message to someone for whom the message was not intended? It's illegal in the state of Arizona. It's a felony to fake a telephone message. It's a felony to cut hair without a license or sell less than five turnips in a bunch or conceal a horse you ran over and killed with your car. And by God you better not commit adultery or conduct a raffle or write an anonymous letter that encourages distrust in another person. It's all against the law."

"Looks like we'll need a good lawyer," Alice said. "Or a judge we can pay off."

"What you need, you slut, is a whipping." He smoked his cigarillo, flexing that tattoo on his arm, the hula girl drawn forties style — Betty Boop — the ink faded now. "A whupping, I should say. A good old-fashioned whupping. That's it. That's what you need."

The sunlight was heavy on my forehead and arms and I had to squint against the sparkle off the pool. Alice strolled down the steps into the water and took his head into her hands and kissed him. He sputtered and shoved her back so she half-fell, half-sat on the concrete deck, legs splayed in the pool. One of her sandals came loose and floated.

"You're psycho," he said.

"So we're still on good terms."

"No more of that kissing on the lips. Or I'll have to take action."

"I was just saying hello."

"Then say it and get out. And take him with you."

She fished for her sandal and tied it on, then let her foot down in the water again and kicked slow little waves. "You remember Roy."

The Judge tugged his hat lower over his eyes. "Roy, I'd have a lot more respect for you if you'd fucked her in the ring. Most men I know would have. Most men I run around with, that is. You had to wait and do it in private. You had to pull the drapes and keep the light off and your eyes closed."

I knew just how to play him: macho. "You want a report?"

"What are you ashamed of? Damn right, I want a report."

"We went to her trailer and she took everything you'd given her and put it in a pile and burned it. We went to my place and fucked all night long and during breakfast and we stopped on the way out here and fucked at high noon in the bed of her pickup."

"She burned it all, eh? Sorry I missed that. The trailer too?"

"The trailer's still there. It would've made too much of a mess."

"I wish she had torched it. For the insurance, I wish she had. It's falling down anyway."

"You'll have to torch it yourself."

"I guess so. You wouldn't do the job for me, Roy? Roy what?"

"McDonnell."

"You're somewhat easier to understand without a noose around your neck. So tell me something. What the hell are you doing here, Roy?"

"I'm down from Albuquerque to pick up a fighting dog or two."

"I see. It's dogs you're interested in. Who do you know up in Albuquerque? Somebody who's into dogs? You know King Bowie?"

"No."

"Frankie Larson?"

"No. I don't know anyone."

"I see. We're back to keeping the drapes closed and the lights off."

"I run a couple of quick-photo shops up there, that's all."

"Roy's quick-photos and quick-fucks and quick-torch-jobs."

"She torched it, but I got a kick out of watching it burn. It all belonged to you, didn't it?"

"Roy's simulated tough," Alice said.

The Judge liked that one. He ate an ice cube out of his glass. He should have thrown us out, and then we'd have had a chance. But he just said, "Maybe I overreacted last night. Alice has a problem she needs help with. I try to help her. You hold a grudge?"

I told him, "No. We're just getting to know each other."

"You take my Alice, might as well drink my whiskey." He tossed the bottle to me. I had to swig it and toss the bottle back to him. "You don't know her well, do you, Roy?"

"About as well as you do, I guess."

"I doubt that. I seriously doubt that."

"I connected with her up in Laughlin. She brought me luck, so I stayed connected. I'm surprised I didn't run into you up there."

"You a gambling man?"

"I'll take a few chances."

"I realize that. And now you imagine she can help you

luck onto a dog? And in return you'll help fuck her in the back
of that pickup. What'd she tell you about me?"

"She fell for your tattoo. Then she showed me where you
stubbed out your smokes on her belly."

"I did that? She told you?"

"I showed him," Alice said. "See?"

The Judge didn't look at her. "I don't sound like a very
nice fellow, do I? Maybe you shouldn't be here risking my
temper."

"Dogs. It's as simple as that. I saw your Devil working last
night."

"He's not for sale."

"Maybe I'll settle for one of your others. One that has his
bloodline. Maybe you can teach me a little something about
dogfighting."

"Teach? What can any man teach another?" The Judge
uncapped the whiskey bottle, emptied it into his glass, and
threw the bottle into the pool. He drank from the glass and
made a face. "You can hold a chickenfight at the mall or at
halftime of your high school football game or on the church
lawn every Sunday morning between services. But dogfighting is illegal in the state of Arizona."

"You were saying, just about everything is. That doesn't
stop it."

"Laws don't stop anything. They just help us control the
chaos and hold some people responsible." He swigged from
his glass and threw it into the pool too. "I detect a disrespect-
ful tone in your voice that I don't like. The law may be too
much of a nanny sometimes, and there are individual cases
where it's all right to break any law. In my years on the bench
I saw victims who had it coming, who were begging to be
beaten or robbed or fucked against their will or even mur-
dered. But there are benefits to our system that you appar-

ently don't understand. Take me and my harmless hobby.
Even with my record, my long years of service to the law, I'd
rather not get hauled into court for dogfighting, and that
makes me cautious. Now you want to get to know me and my
dogs. The only references you have are Alice here, and the
fact that you've got the balls to face me after last night. Of the
two the second impresses me more. You might be a dogfighter after all. You see how the law acts on dogfighting,
Roy? Quality control. If there wasn't a law against dogfighting then anyone could get into it, you wouldn't have to have
balls or be sharp at all, and there would go the whole sport. It
would be as bad as boxing, look at all the chumps who don't
even last a round in a championship fight. As long as dogfighting is against the law, people who aren't qualified will
get busted or scared out, and I for one hope they do. It's the
same with everything from simple assault to grand theft to
murder one. Respect the law, Roy, even if you have to break
it — understand how it establishes quality control."

He swished his arm through the water, raised it. "You see
this watch? It isn't waterproof. I don't give a fuck. I've had it
dunked most of the night and it's still ticking." He stared at
the watch, the leather band that was soaked and dark, the
fogged face. "Try to bullshit me, Roy, and you're out of here.
The details have to hold up. You've got five seconds to tell me
the most terrible thing you ever did."

The old screwballer.

"One . . ."

Shit.

"Three . . . Four . . . Five."

He tapped his watch. "Adios, Roy." He yelled to the
house, "Ed! Hey, Ed! Got some trash needs throwing out."

"Hold on — what's it going to take?" Guts knotted, I
found my sunglasses, slid them on, and started to talk, still

not certain what I'd pick out, how far I'd go, trying to cut him with every word. Telling myself, it's Roy's story anyway.

"I saw some kids drown . . ."

"Details!"

"It was a lake up in Colorado. They called it Pleasant Lake then, maybe they call it something else now. Seven, eight years ago, middle of winter, it was fucking cold. I was up there . . . doing a brochure for one these programs that try to cure big-city punks with a dose of wilderness. A bunch of kids were marching on the ice. One kid broke through, then a couple more. The ice was rotten. Some counselors tried to pull them out and they broke through . . . I was on shore, with some others in the snowdrifts — we couldn't do anything. Anybody who tried went under. They splashed around shouting for help and trying to pull themselves out, and the ice kept breaking. By the time a rescue crew got there, they'd sunk out of sight . . . It took a week for the divers to fish out the eight bodies . . ."

The words stopped coming. The Judge stared at me and let the silence pile up. "Is that it?"

"I took pictures of all of it."

Alice clapped once and I almost snapped. "I like your story, Roy."

The Judge ignored her. "Reasonably terrible . . . It's not like you're a serial killer or a savings-and-loan shyster."

He stood up, dripping water off his sunburn and his sixty-four-year-old paunch and his blue bikini trunks. "I'll show you dogs." He adjusted his hat and marched up the steps out of the pool and into the house. Devil came out of the water and began to nuzzle Alice and lick her, acting like a big puppy. That's the other side of these pit bulls — when they're not ripping things up, they're goofy to be your friend, more so than most any other dog — but no matter

how much tail-wagging and licking goes on it's hard to relax
around one wondering when it might suddenly come with
the teeth. Emergency rooms make a living off people who
play with pit bulls, because they can seem so lovable right
up until the moment they're not. Right now Devil was a pup
with Alice.

The dog yard was a hundred yards off in the desert, where
the training could go on in private. There was a clearing with
exercise contraptions and a kennel run and a formation of
steel stakes driven into the dirt. The pit bulls were chained
to the stakes, spaced apart so they couldn't rip into each
other. When the Judge got dressed and took us out there the
pit bulls started lunging at us, trying to be friendly, or to rip
us, or both. Some of them were chained on half-inch steel
cable strung like clothesline, so they could sprint back and
forth and maximize each lunge. The Judge had Devil on a
choke chain, and Devil did his own lunging at all the others,
wheezing as the chain cut off his air, and lunging harder. So
of course the Judge started in with a lecture on how wonder-
ful the breed was.

"They don't bark. They don't bristle. They don't bluff.
They attack, without a thought about being hurt or killed or
whether they're good dogs or bad. They're streamlined,
merciless, efficient. All the virtues of the modern world, and
none of the ambiguities. People say they're uncontrollable.
It's not true. If anything they're too controllable. They've
been bred for one thing and it's all they care about, killing.
Put it another way, winning."

There were maybe a dozen of these pit bulls of every color
but all with the same mean eyes, snapping and wheezing on
their chains and digging their paws into the dirt, and another
dozen in the kennels hurling themselves against the wire

mesh trying to get at us. Here and there some of them were just waiting, intently, for us to come within range.

Of course he had them named after famous lawyers. "That's F. Lee Bailey over there, and Kuntsler, and Darrow, and Roy Cohn. When I watch them fight, it's just like I was back in court. These pit bulls know how to cross-examine. Right now they want to cross-examine my Devil. They know he's top dog. He'd take them all on." The Judge tugged Devil over to one of the cable clotheslines and chained him there with a padlock. He shook his head. "People'll steal anything, especially a good pit bull." Once Devil was chained the others eased off. Some of them started wagging their tails, and we had to pet them. "It's like with any dog. Don't let them know you're afraid."

Alice walked in among the dogs, letting them jump all over her. After a while, I risked it.

10

WE GOT the real pit bull tour that afternoon, and over the next couple of weeks. The Judge opened up to us, to me, and I thought it was just payback for me opening up to him, boosted by ego and hormones — his desire to impress Alice and play the master of pit-bulldom. He gave us all the pretty facts, about how pit bulls bite down with almost a ton per square inch of pressure, and how they're descended from the distinguished line of English butcher dogs that were bred for ignoring pain and locking onto a bull's nose so the butcher could move in with his skull hammer, and how dogfighting originated as the fine old sport of baiting bulls and bears, when they'd throw a pack of dogs in the ring against a lone bigger animal and make bets on how long it would take, and even going way back to when the Greeks and Romans had their war dogs, and sicced them after wild animals and competing armies, ranks of war dogs marching into battle, armored and with teeth bared.

"War dogs," the Judge told us. "That's what pit bulls really are, that's why so many people desire them — for aggression, for protection, everybody's into that. Pit bulls against paranoia. But too many people are into pit bulls now, and most of them don't know what they're doing, they're breeding dogs that aren't game, they're breeding losers, dogs that back away from a fair fight but will take after children and old ladies, and the whole thing is getting a bad name. The most important rule about pit bulls is don't let the losers live, don't let them breed. Once the dogs got popular, once they got to be an American breed, people lost track of that simple rule."

And we got the demonstrations, one pit bull after another leaping up high to lock its teeth on a limb of a mesquite that was already chewed up, and then dangling there from its jaws, twenty, thirty, forty-five minutes until it dropped off from exhaustion, sometimes passed out, but with increased jaw power. One pit bull after another on the treadmill, running all out, hour after hour after hour, lured on by a dead cat or a kitten in a mesh sack suspended inches ahead. The Judge treadmilled his best dogs eight hours and then tossed them the cat as a reward. On the wheel, a spoked iron thing set up parallel to the ground, a cat would be chained to one spoke, and a pit bull chained to the spoke behind would run around and around all day until it got the reward. Sometimes the cats were live, and that made the pit bulls try harder. Sometimes the reward was a chicken or a rooster or a puppy or a terrier or minipoodle. The Judge had all sorts of dog bait, and all sorts of secrets.

"Keep your pit bulls dry before a fight. Run them and run them some more, and be stingy with their water. Keep them hot. Notice how there isn't any shade around here? Dehydrate them and thicken their blood, and when they get cut in the ring, bleeding will be minimal. Lean them down, so there's no loose skin that can be grabbed and torn. They'll stay at fighting weight on a diet of liquid protein. This is the brand to use."

And we got to see some rolls, the practice fights, where

the Judge let two of his pit bulls go at it, or somebody else
brought a pit bull over to take on one of his for fine-tuning.
There was no crowd and no betting and they didn't let the
dogs go all out, just held them on leashes and eased them
together until they were joined by bites. Then after maybe
an hour they pried the dogs apart with what they call breaking sticks — just shove the stick in your pit bull's mouth and
get some leverage and pry until its lips are bleeding, and
keep prying until it lets go. The longer it holds on against the
breaking stick, the better pit bull it is.

"Get that stick in there. Twist now. Harder. Harder. Pull.
Hear him crying? That's not from the pain. Not this dog. He
just absolutely doesn't want to give up. He's refusing to let
go. Hear him cry? Pull. Twist on that stick. Pull. I got him.
He's game. He's game."

All the while Alice urged the Judge on: Show us this, show
us that, tell us that awful story again, you awful man. It was
just a come-on, just her act. The Judge didn't go for it, but he
did like having her around. I didn't see the significance. For
once I wasn't even seeing her, not as a woman, the way she
wanted to be seen. All I was seeing were those terrible pit
bulls, hanging in trees, snapping after dead cats, chewing
into each other. I could just about feel them chewing into me,
and sometimes, Alice would let her act slip, and for a moment
in that heat she'd be shivering. Those dogs.

I shot as much as I could, which was a lot, using the tiny
spy camera that I could hold in one palm and shoot just
waving my hand, then tuck it back in my pocket. I had
disguises for the camera — a belt-buckle rig and a bogus
cigarette pack — that I'd tried on other jobs, but they were
hard to aim and seemed like tired gimmicks that might go
wrong or be discovered. I preferred the looseness of the
sleight of hand, the expressive gesture, the rush of: in your

face! Alice ran a constant diversion, the men were watching
her, not me, and there were so many redundant oppor-
tunities to shoot that I didn't have to take huge chances. I
could stray off or turn my back or tie my shoe or even cough
and snap a shot like any gunslinger and get off on the
movement and the flourish. With each shot I had the Judge
nailed even tighter along with his two flunkies who helped
train the dogs — the sick-eyed Ed Dempsey and the weedy
longhaired redneck, L. R. Greer. Lunchtimes the three of
them and Alice and I sat down at the long table in the ranch
dining room and a Mexican woman named Luisa served us
Big Ed's hand-squeezed lemonade and some version of beef
and beans, the Arizona delicacies. Once we even stayed
over for dinner and had a simulated good time drinking the
Judge's twenty-year-old whiskey and watching cop-
liberation TV and the quiz show where they have all the
answers and you're supposed to guess the questions. They
happened to have a column on Charlie Dickens quotes, and
Big Ed got every one: "What's 'Bring in the bottled lightning, the clean tumbler and a corkscrew!'?" . . . "What's
'You'll find us rough, sir, but you'll find us ready!'?" . . .
"What's 'It's a mad world. Mad as Bedlam.'?" And we went
through the usual scenes, Big Ed taking me aside to demonstrate how he pressed his lemons: "I don't know who you
are or what you're up to, but you smell like just before a rain
to me. Watch yourself. You louse up the Judge, and I'll
make thin lemonade out of you. *Comprende?*" Later on the
other one volunteered an explanation of his name: "L.R. —
stands for Larry the Rat. That's what all my friends call
me." And of course we got to sit on the big couch uphol-
stered entirely in rattlesnake skins. We went with L.R. to
take a load of dead dogs and cats and other used-up dog bait

out into the desert, to what L.R. called the dog dump, and I got shots of that mash too. I shot another round of dogfighting at the old barn way out south, where once again Devil did his cross-examination very efficiently. Every night when we were through with the dogs I'd take Alice back into the city and drop her at the Paradise Motel. I had to ignore her looks, the little outfits she'd bought, and the moves she did by rote — the way she touched me here and there. I'd go down to the paper late and develop the day's film with Rissler hovering over my shoulder and Suzy Kino to avoid. The things I'll do for a story.

After that I'd go home to drink myself to sleep, as if tequila might drive all of it out of my mind. One night Rissler had to come home with me. The story was close to breaking, and of course he had to be my buddy when it did. He had to be right on top of it, and me, to get as much of the credit as he could. We sat in my place doing the routine, downing shots and sucking limes and licking salt, with the cooler blasting on high and the windows and door wide open onto the little rectangle of summer-killed grass and the deserted sidewalk and street. We looked through the dog photos for the umpteenth time, and Rissler got all excited for the umpteenth time, and then we had to invent something to talk about, so we settled important journalistic questions like: Would the business office shell out if I had to buy one of the Judge's fighting pit bulls?

"Can you see the expense form on that?" Rissler said. "Or the IRS's reaction when we try to deduct it? 'Trained fighting pit bull, two thousand dollars, business expense.' We better wrap this thing up without having to buy a dog."

We covered all the angles, even admitting to ourselves how, technically, we were invading the Judge's privacy by taking after him on his own property with a camera. This just gave Rissler a chance to stand tall.

"Let the bastard sue us. The publicity will just pull more people into the story. Even if he beats us in court, we look tougher for it. Nobody will care about a technicality like that once they see what he's doing to these dogs. We went after these photos, we were willing to take the risk for a greater good. Here's to the greater good." And he did a shot.

"Macky, in a few months we'll be off this rag and onto a real paper. This undercover job is a hot-dog stunt so we won't be going to the *New York Times*. Not the *New York Times*." He exaggerated the name. "The *New York Times* never did a story this interesting. They never did one this hot. But the *Washington Post* might go for it, and go for the guys who did it. Or the *Miami Herald*. The *Philadelphia Inquirer.* The papers that own the Pulitzer for investigative reporting. One of them should pick us up. Hell, they'll be bidding for us."

I didn't like Rissler laying it out like that, not because it wasn't some of what I was thinking, but because he was horning in, and nobody wants their ambitions stated so clearly. I said, "Let's stick to the greater good," and had a shot.

Rissler waved his glass. "There's only two kinds of journalism: nasty, and incompetent."

"You mean incontinent."

"Yes, that's exactly what I mean, decrepit and leaking piss. About the only way we could improve this story would be to make it nastier. We could give it a little more oomph. Like getting the Judge or one of his boys to strangle you again. It was one of them that tried before, wasn't it? You told me it was her but she was just mixed up in it. You couldn't arrange a replay, so we could get it on the record, could you?

That would make a good story a great one. That would guarantee a wide readership."

"You've had demographic studies done on that?"

"Why sure — anytime a reporter gets strangled, the readers love it. They buy extra copies and send some to their relatives. The advertisers love it too."

"And the Pulitzer board."

"Sure — they love it when a journalist suffers for his story." And I had to give him five.

"For the greater good," we said together. We went late with the tequila routine, because that was our role. We watched ourselves sitting there playing it.

This was the real world and something had to break down, and finally it did. The next morning Alice wasn't waiting for me in front of the Paradise Motel. I parked and went up to her room. She was a while answering my knock, and then, asking, "Who is it?" she sounded weary.

"Macky. Let's get a move on."

She cracked the door as far as the chain lock. "You alone?"

"As ever."

She undid the chain and let me see all of her. She was back in my old shorts and T-shirt. For Alice that was her nun costume. She'd been worked over pretty good. She had a split lip and a black eye and dried blood in her nose and scratches and bruises here and there. She didn't want me studying her. The room had been worked over too, furniture knocked around, a lamp busted, the bedcovers yanked off. A set of handcuffs dangled from one of her wrists, one cuff locked on her, the other cuff locked and empty.

"You were getting to be such pals," she said. "Man to man. Pretending. He followed me here last night. He barged in and locked me in these and did this. The Judge and his hard-on, on a spree. I got a hand loose and fought him. Made noise. He had to leave. He didn't get anything."

She asked, "Where were you, Macky? Shouldn't you be taking notes? How about some photos?" She tried to pose with one hand behind her head, but the loose cuff swung in her face and she lowered the hand. "I'm going to kill him."

11

PEOPLE threaten it all the time in Arizona, for being cut off in traffic or subjected to loud music, or to settle all the other serious offenses. As worked-over as she was, she had more justification to follow through than plenty of them who do. So I put my arms around her and tried to move her mind off murder. She shoved me and scratched my cheek with the cuffs and twisted away, and she said it again, "He's going to die and I'm going to watch it."

She asked, "You ever watch a man die from up close?"

"Stop it," I told her.

Her eyes were glittering from something deep down inside her that should have stayed hidden.

"That's it for your story, Macky. This is off the record now."

"The hell with the story."

She held her hands down at her sides and started crying. I went for her again and she collapsed into me and cried. Of course I couldn't help noticing how we fit together, how she felt against me, how surprisingly vulnerable she seemed again. I tried to ease her away from me down on the bed, and she said, "That's where he put me." She sagged onto the nightstand and knocked off the phone and leaned over her

knees and clasped her hands over her head, hiding her face
with her hair. She cried awhile. Then she let me give her a
drink of water from a plastic cup I broke out of its seal of
freshness, and I cleaned traces of blood off her. The crying
had softened her looks.

"The job's done, Macky. We don't have to put up with
each other anymore."

"That's up to us."

"Don't worry about me. Don't be weak."

"I do worry, Alice."

We went on like that, her pulling me in, and me going
along and thinking, it's about time. I tried to stop thinking
that. The walls and what had happened inside them were
pressing us together. Maybe she'd wanted it just like this, the
way she'd come on to the Judge and to me. Her fingers cut
into my arm. I got her up and walked her to the door.

"Where're we going?" she asked. She was dreamy. I took
her out and down the back stairs and got her into my car
without anyone noticing the cuffs dangling off her wrist.

"Somewhere cool," I said. I drove us across the city and
got on the two-lane that winds in a hurry to the summit of the
dominant range, the Santa Catalina Mountains. In Arizona a
lot of the mountains are named after saints, as if up on top
there'll be blessed relief from the heat and all the trouble
down below. It works for the heat anyway.

"It'll be better up there," I told her. "Trees, and shade
you can lie in. Not at all like down here."

She didn't say anything. She leaned back in the seat with
that dreamy look on her battered face. We took the curves
and drove higher, out of the desert and into the piñon and
juniper, and then the bigger pines. I began to wonder just
what I was doing, but I didn't want to wonder too hard. I had

told her the hell with the story, and I was trying to get over that too. The research was done — she was right about that.

She got less dreamy when I made the pitch. "Forget it. I'm not whining to the cops or anybody else about being roughed up, and if you put it in your story I'll say you made it up. I'll say you made up everything. I'm not climbing in the geek cage so you can sell papers or ads or your career or whatever else you want to sell. This is between the Judge and me."

"I'm in this too."

"How far, newspaperman? You got a gun?"

I didn't understand her, not then. I thought her talk about killing was desire for revenge combined with that Arizona-style youthful exuberance. "I'm talking about nailing him so tight he might as well be dead and buried. Without you the only victims we got are dogs. You're the human interest. Everybody can relate to what he did to you."

"What do you relate to, Macky?"

"Using everything we got on this guy."

"That's what I'm talking about."

"Alice, you keep saying I'm simulated tough. I'll turn it around on you. You ever watch a man die?"

She just got that dreamy look again. "Being cynical is what you can afford, isn't it, Macky? It makes you good at your job, because everybody else seems like they're faking it, and a lot of them are. I talk about how things are simulated, you get it wham bam. You think you're a mile back from everything. If you admitted that you hate yourself, you'd have to admit you're still alive . . . You're the jack with the hidden eye. You do man-and-the-challenge to prove you're untouchable, you're not scared or made of flesh, but it's really the only way you can feel anything, by torquing

yourself, and you're desperate to do it. You go around looking for shock therapy. *Zzzzzzap.* That's all I am to you.
That's — "

"That's all you want to be."

"You can't even make it sound like a complaint. Want
another jolt? I'm supposed to believe you're in this for a story.
Like, you're doing good . . . It's more like this, newspaperman: Every time you nail somebody, you're nailing yourself."

She glared at me. "Do me a favor. Have the guts to shut
the fuck up."

The countryside reeled by. We were close to the sky and it
had darkened from blue to black. One of the summer thun-
derstorms that collect over the mountains was going to break
right down on top of us. Black clouds were piling up. People
had pulled off at picnic tables scattered under the pines.
Where the road ended we stopped and got out at an overlook.
The wind had picked up. It was chilly for the first time in
months. Some of the clouds dragged along below us and we
couldn't see the desert or the city. Alice hugged herself and
stared at the clouds. The weather was threatening everybody
down off the mountain. I got her back in the car and we
started down.

"I don't want to go back yet," she said. "I want to feel the
storm."

I pulled into a picnic ground where they had ramadas over
the tables and some with concrete fireplaces. A mist was
blowing. We got damp and then wet walking to our table. A
family had built a fire at one of the other ramadas and the kids
were running around picking raspberries before the rain got
heavier. Alice stood out in the open with her hair blowing.
Her face was dripping and the soaked shirt was an almost
transparent skin on her curves. We seemed to be starting all

over. The split on her lip had reopened and was glistening
with fresh blood. She walked close to me, staring, and swung
her hands behind her back, wormed her shoulders and elbows.

"I don't have a key," she said.

She turned around to show me she'd worked her free hand
into the cuffs. She waved her fingers at me down low and
snicked the cuffs as tight as they'd go and then faced me.

"I have another challenge for you, Macky."

"You trying to get me arrested?"

"Kiss me, Macky. Kiss me or I'll scream. I'll scream and
keep on screaming until someone comes and then I'll tell
them you did this to me. Because I hate you too, Macky, for
what you've thought of me from the beginning. Because it
wouldn't cost me anything."

She shouted, "Macky!" and the people at the other table
looked at us. I got between her and them and she began to
scream, "Help!" faintly and then louder. I grabbed her like
we were embracing and clamped a hand over her mouth and
she struggled against me and bit me, screaming now down in
her throat. I pressed my lips on hers. She kissed me and
fought me with her shoulders and kissed me harder and
wedged her knee up between my legs. She would have fallen
if I hadn't held her up. I broke off the kiss and she panted
into my neck. "Take off my shirt," she said. I walked us
deeper into the ramada and against the concrete wall. "Take
it off!" she yelled, "Take — " and I had to peel the shirt up
over her head and down her arms behind her where it wadded
against the cuffs. Her nipples were fine-lined by the rain that
was blowing in harder now. "Feel me, Macky," she said, and
I cupped my hands on her breasts. She tipped back her head
as I did what she said. "Take off everything. Feel me all
over." Her shorts had buttons that held me up, then I had

them undone and off her slowly rotating hips, and I tugged
down her panties. Car doors slammed. The other car was
leaving. "Lay me down on the table." I did everything she
said under the rain that was loud on the roof of the ramada. It
sounded just like the crowd that night at the dogfight, and I
think she heard it too, cheering and urging us on.

That's how it is in the desert, either bone-dry or flash
flood.

I'm not saying it made sense. I'm not saying anything,
except that at the time, there didn't seem to be any choice.
Not after she'd called me out so accurately. Not with the rain
demanding that from us, and the cuffs closing off any escape.
It was our way of telling everything and everybody to go to
hell, and of telling each other that too — she had been hating
me all along, because I was a man I guess, and I wound up
taking her for every man there ever was. I could show her
something about nailing myself. I didn't want it to be that
way, but on one level, it was — a real Arizona courtship, and
those cuffs were our engagement rings.

Afterward she lay on top of me. She started nuzzling me
and biting me and teasing me with that little scream and
pretty soon I had to roll her off the table and out into the rain
and the pine needles and mud and we went at it again. She
was locked in those cuffs with the chill tightening her skin
and every muscle, and her hair wild in the rain. She was
exactly and totally what I wanted.

Yeah, Macky, yeah.

It wasn't just sex, it was crashing limits. The jump, and
the rush — it was everything she'd accused me of. No woman
had ever connected with me like that, drawing me in and
draining me the way she did. I couldn't stop myself, really, I
had never been able to with her. Something about the way

she looked, so knowing, the way she posed herself, always cocked and ready to fire, the way she left nothing to doubt when she moved. Naked she was a morsel, not a straight line on her, with all the tucks and hollows that drive a man wild. The way her bare calf rounded out and curved in behind her knee. The teasing now-you-see-it, now-you-don't definition of the long muscles submerged in her thighs. The dimples low on her back, where her spine arched into her rump. The deep hollows along her collarbones, and the softness slung below. All aching to be explored. That broken nose making her look just a little bit tough, the dark eyes daring you to make something of it. And, and, and. Oh, she had me all right, and she knew what to do. She was a whore or just a woman who liked to do it, or maybe she liked the power it gave her over a man, I didn't care, the result was the same for me. I just had to be careful not to lose myself in her. I had to keep my mind on the story. You can guess how easy that was.

Eventually we were just cold and wet and aware of what we'd done — and what it might lead to. I tugged her clothes around her and we started driving with the heater on. Her teeth were chattering. I got out the blanket I'd wrapped her in the night she'd burned all the Judge's stuff, and wrapped her in it again.

"My whole life is an emergency," she said.

"Can't you work out of those cuffs like you did before?"

"No. Just the one was loose, and I fixed that. I didn't want you to have an out."

"I didn't, did I? If you'd kept on screaming sooner or later a mob would have been on me like I was Jack the Ripper himself. They're always looking for Jack the Ripper. They would've come in a mob with the torches and guns and the

yellow ribbons or whatever, and they wouldn't've been interested in what I had to say. You locked me into it all right."

"Who was it giving as good as he got?" She let out her
little-girl giggle. "Feel me, Macky." I had to reach inside the
blanket and do it while she squirmed.

Because of distractions like that it took us a while to get
down the mountain. The rain had been going long and hard
enough to reach the desert, and it beat on the car. The
washes and rivers were running full, the streets were flooded,
and tree branches had blown down. It's either the sun or the
rain punishing you in Arizona. I drove to the Paradise Motel.
She had gotten moody.

"Thanks for the swell time," she said. She backed against
the door and fumbled with the handle and I had to grab her
again.

"Goddamn you, Alice. I'm tempted to let you go."

"That would be a scene. 'Excuse me, desk clerk, are
there any messages? Perhaps somebody dropped off a key for
these handcuffs.' Then what are we doing here? I won't go
back to that room and wait for the Judge to come calling
again. Not unless I have a gun."

"You don't need any gun, so stop talking about it."

I left her in the car and went in and collected her things.
When I came out, of course, who was plunked next to her?

12

I HAD TO LAUGH. I kept on laughing, softly, and shaking my head while I threw her things in back and squeezed in front with both of them, and started driving.

"He just got in," Alice said. "Wasn't anything I could do about it."

"Not like that she can't." Fucking Rissler.

The blanket had slipped down, or he had pulled it off her. She had to lean forward because of the cuffs.

"Don't pay any attention to these," she said. "It's nothing, really."

"Oh?" Rissler said.

I stopped laughing and said, "What do you want?"

He leered. "What do *I* want? Not much. Not much at all. I was looking for you, Macky, because I decided it's time to wrap up this story. You remember the story. We were talking about it last night. I want to share my decision with you . . . That's what I want."

"Is this guy your editor or something?" Alice asked.

"Yes, I am," Rissler said. "For the time being."

"Can't you talk to Macky at the office?"

"The newsroom," Rissler said. "That's what we call it.

That's the business we're in. You have any news for me, Macky?"

"No."

"I would have thought you did. I would have thought you had a lot of news. How about you? Alice Malone, is it? Do you have any news?"

"No. Nothing you can put in the paper."

"Why don't you just tell me what the hell is going on and let me decide if it goes in the paper or not."

"The Judge beat her up last night," I said. "He put the cuffs on her but she got loose."

"She isn't loose now," Rissler said.

"I was showing Macky how it happened," Alice said. "We went up on the mountain. We got wet."

"You certainly did," Rissler said.

"Cut it out," I told him. "You've heard the explanation. Where can I drop you?"

"I'll just ride along. Just take me wherever you're going, Macky. It's not often I get to see a top investigative journalist in action." He asked Alice, "What do you do when your nose itches?"

"I get somebody to scratch it," she said.

I braked and jammed us against the curb. "Get out, Rissler. This doesn't concern you. This isn't going in the story."

"It might," he said.

I reached around Alice and jabbed him. "Get out." I popped his door open and tried to shove him out. I couldn't get any leverage with her in the way and he was resisting. I climbed out my side and ran around the car and hauled him out. He got ahold of my shirt and yanked me against the car and we had a little news conference yelling into each other's faces in the rain.

"I don't give a damn what you do to her," he said. "Not if she likes it. But if you fuck me out of this story you're finished in newspapers. I'll see to that. You won't land a job on a podunk weekly doing obits and leash-law violations."

"I'm not fucking you out of anything. It's my story. You're just along for the ride."

"Hot shit Macky. How many editors would back you like I do? How many would put up with you? I could fire you right now."

"Fine. Then tear up those dogfight photos."

"Macky and his libido. Is that what this's turned into? Get rid of her!"

"Shut up!" I had to give him something else to think about. So I sprung it on him. "I've figured out how to go all the way on this story. How to take it to the max. Are you interested? Get the hell out of here and come by my place in an hour."

I threw him away from me and we stood there in the rain, him mulling over his range of responses, the emotions warring on his face. Finally he composed himself and said, "Okay, I'll be there. And it better be good."

He walked off in the rain and I got the car moving again.

"I thought you two were going to claw each other's eyes out," Alice said. "What did he want?"

"He wants me to get rid of you."

She slumped against the door. I should've felt sick, vile and exposed, and the only protection from it was to not look back, to keep charging. I stroked her nearest leg, around the knee and up and down. She said, "Maybe you should."

"Hell, we're just getting to know each other." I made my fingers into the little newspaperman and walked him up her leg. She crossed her legs and clamped my hand there.

I took us to my place and hustled her inside in the blanket. She watched me haul out my toolbox and then I got behind her to try the nippers and then the vise grips and hacksaw on the cuffs. The cutting turned into a job. She pulled away and faced me.

"We should leave them on. I don't know if I can trust you once you've disposed of the evidence."

"Evidence of what? Trust me to what?"

"To feel me whenever I want it. To do what I say, or else."

"I can't imagine declining an invitation to one of your picnics."

"That's not the same."

I spun her around and nicked her in a few places getting the cuffs off.

"Prove it," she said. And I did.

After all that there was a natural letdown and when she got up to take a shower I was left alone with another thought I couldn't get rid of — that it was all wrong, it wasn't going to work out, and would only get worse if I didn't spring up and push her out the door right then. But as high as she'd taken me, I had to come down somewhere and be somebody, I had to center on something, and of course that was as a journalist on his story. That was my safe little groove, she was right about that along with most everything else. So right and then so wrong — the alluring contradiction. I'd have to see which side of her won. And which side of me . . . The story, Macky. Obsess on that. Keep charging. This is the dogfight, on every acre and in the newsroom and in bed, it's all the ring — and you better protect your neck or you'll be belly up before you know it.

The real stories summed up the world.

I'd have to get Rissler to go along with it. We'd joked around it the other night. This story was about a lot more than a bunch of savage dogs. We needed to humanize it and give it some oomph and take it to the max. So what if, all along, it seemed that meant taking her to the max?

I had ideas.

I found her crying in the shower and that's what finally did it. She was leaning against the tile wall, her face screwed, with the water and tears flowing down her. The water had gone cold. Seeing her like that, all dusky against the white tiles, showing all the scratches and bruises and those three old cigarillo scars burned into her, I wanted to hurt the Judge like he'd hurt her. I wanted his face under my fists — hell, under my boots. I got her out of the shower and into my robe and gave her some tequila. She winced and had some more.

"I'm not crying because of you, Macky."

"I know that."

"It's him. I can't get him out of my mind."

I held her and stroked her hair and she calmed down and nestled in my arms.

"What are we going to do about the Judge, Macky?"

"The story."

"He'll be embarrassed and that's about it. It's just journalism."

"Just journalism. I'll try to remind myself. Remember when I told you there was more to it? This is what there is. We'll nail him."

"He'll track us down and take it out on us."

"They'll charge him with dogfighting."

"That'll just make him another good ol' boy. Face it, Macky. No story goes far enough."

*　　*　　*

There was a knock on the door and I let Rissler in. He had changed to dry clothes and a nylon jacket. It was still raining. Night had set in. He looked at Alice in my robe.

"She's staying here tonight," I told him.

"If nobody tells me about it, I can't object."

"So nobody told you."

"I'll go for a walk," Alice said. "Since you're being such a sport." She took some of her things into the bathroom and came out dressed in jeans and a halter top. She held out her hand and Rissler took off his jacket and gave it to her and she put it on.

He told her, "Make it a long walk. There's some cash in the pocket. Get yourself a decent meal. Or a decent drink. If you can find one."

"If Macky makes the same pitch to you as he did to me, I won't do it," she said. "I won't let you use how I was roughed up. I'm not inviting your subscribers into my private life."

"With your private life, I don't blame you."

She kissed me and put some English on it for him and left. Rissler said, "Just get to it."

He had to act like it was another difficult and critical deliberation on his long list. I was jittery, pacing the room while I laid it out: "This isn't anything from journalism school. They don't debate it at any conferences. It's what we were joking about — the hole in this story. On top of dogs we've got people tearing into each other and we need to document that. The Judge had me dog-poled and just about got her and me lynched at the first dogfight — " Rissler started to interrupt but I overrode him. "So I didn't give you all the details, that's what happened, and now he's escalated from humiliation to working her over, and all we have on the record against him is a little dogfighting. That's all we have pictures of. We don't have him trashing people. We can write

up what happened, but we haven't got any proof, and Alice
might be so pissed off at us, she'd deny it. So where would
we be then? This should be clear and unambiguous. I want
the big bad Judge escalating against me. Let him get physi-
cal. Only this time it'll be our setup, with witnesses, pictures, the works."

"Great. We'll swing by his place right now and let them
have at you. I'll set up a lawn chair and spectate."

"Whatever you want. We'll tip him off about who I am,
what I've been doing, let him think he might be able to stop
the story if he takes me out. He might tell himself that's the
reason, but he'll do it because it's personal now, between him
and me with Alice in between. He's got the temper for it."

"You're fucking crazy! First the handcuffs and now a little
beating?"

"You wouldn't like some photos of the Judge pulling some
shit like this?" He just stared at me, not shocked anymore,
starting to see how it might come down — already halfway
willing to agree, but having to play responsible. I told him,
"You wouldn't like to see me taking a few punches?" Letting
him know he'd be there too, getting some glory. "When I was
shooting *San Ignacio Blues*, Jimmy Santos got his arm broken
for it. Now Alice has gotten it. I'm taking my own lumps
from now on."

"And well you should! Get on the violins!" Coming
around. "It's too dangerous. Why wouldn't he just kill you?
Maybe he wouldn't . . . he hasn't yet that we know of. Christ,
after you got out of the hospital, they'd probably throw us
both in jail."

"Not how I've got it figured."

"And just how is that?"

I worked on him, not that he needed it. He saw how his
career would be guaranteed if we pulled it off. Something

like this can set a journalist up for life. Twenty years later
they'd still be talking it up in the newsrooms. Just like
Rissler had said, they all love it when a journalist suffers for
his story.

I could pretend it didn't have anything to do with nailing
myself. I could be what any journalist should be: objective.

What finally persuaded Rissler was that he'd be able to
play a starring role. He could get the credit for saving me, if it
came to that. That would put him right up there for any
awards, and jobs on bigger papers, and have him in demand
as a featured speaker at all the journalism conferences, as
long as the story behind the story, about how we did it, never
came out.

It didn't take a lot of thinking, and maybe that's something in my defense. I got a yellow pad and we jotted down
a script. Rissler read it in a loud whisper while I recorded
him on my phone machine. He ran through it a couple of
times and then of course he had to do some editing on the
wording and then he ran through it again. We listened to the
playback and picked out the version that sounded the most
convincing. It was nearly nine o'clock by then. I dialed the
Judge at his ranch and when he answered, I played the tape
of Rissler whispering:

"You're being played for a sap. This Roy McDonnell
works for the *News-Gazette*. His real name is Macky and he's
been investigating you and your dogfighting. He's been
laughing his ass off at how dumb you are, and he's been
fucking your Alice. He used to fuck me, you don't need
those details but I just thought you'd like to know. He fucks
his way around. He might even try it on your dogs. If you'd
like to take it up with him, about midnight he'll be nosing
around that old barn out south where you hold the dogfights.

He's planning to take some pictures. He'll be out there all by himself thinking he's got you by the balls."

"I see," the Judge said. "Thank you very much." And he hung up before we did.

"Level-headed bastard, isn't he," Rissler said. "We'll get him on assault charges and put it all in print."

I had to remind him, "A simulated assault."

13

I'VE TRIED to explain why it was necessary. For me, for Alice and Rissler, and to feed the journalism combine that was hungry for a story, a big story. After all, we weren't getting any facts wrong. We weren't trying to make out the Judge was something he wasn't — we were just giving him an opportunity to put it on the record. Sure, I might lose a tooth or two, but once I got bashed there'd be no doubt that I was at the top of the story, instead of Rissler or anyone else. The story would be mine alone. Maybe it wasn't the most honest approach, but it seemed more honest than to go on letting everyone who helped me get beaten up while I played the professional journalist. Sure, I had at least one lofty reason for sandbagging the Judge.

If he didn't come through, I hadn't lost anything. We were ready to go to print anyway. But I thought he'd have to get back at me, the way I had set him up, for his own self-respect, and because this was Arizona.

Alice's pickup rolled up in front of my place. "I walked over to the motel," she said. "Was that far enough?"

"Take it easy," I told her. I was scrounging through my gear for what Rissler and I needed. "I'm going out on a shoot."

"What did he talk you into?"

Rissler answered for me. "Not a great deal."

"I thought we were trusting each other."

"We are on important things," I said. "This is just journalism. Remember?"

I packed the gear in my car. We were taking my car because the Judge would expect it.

"So you're leaving me behind. This is the last time," Alice said. She did the routine. She really could kiss and cling.

Rissler got in the car. "We don't want to be late."

"See you later, Alice."

"Maybe so, Macky."

We drove off. The rain had stopped. Rissler was getting nervous. He stared ahead through the windshield and talked too much. "I'm not wearing the right shoes. Loafers. Maybe we should stop by my place so I can change. I'm not in any kind of shape. Haven't been jogging for six months. God, I don't know about all this."

"It'll be okay."

"A lot of things could go wrong. If anybody finds out how we did it, we're fucked."

"Nobody will."

"It probably won't be too bad. He probably won't even break any bones. Not now that he knows you're a journalist. He'd be the obvious suspect if anything serious happens to you, even if you just disappear. He'll know that. All he'll want to do is teach you a lesson. Maybe it'll cost you some dental work, that's all."

I kept my foot on the gas and that made the roads rougher. We wound over the little mountain range of rocks and down into the empty valley and turned off into the mesquites and ended up at the old leaning-over barn. When I cut the engine and headlights the place seemed deserted. The Judge couldn't have been there already. He had a lot farther to come from his ranch way out east of the city, and our appointment wasn't for another two hours or so. There was no moon and it was black dark.

We had a couple of flashlights and Rissler held one while I pried the padlock off the barn door. The place was ready for more dogfights, with the ring and the stands and the dangling lights, but the power was shut off somewhere. Rissler lit me up while I climbed the stands and jumped up and caught one of the rafters, swung myself up and sat on it. The rafters ran crossways spaced about three feet apart, with the ceiling rising to a peak far above them. There was a loft in one corner, but it looked rickety and there was no ladder, and I didn't want to try it. Rissler passed up a flashlight and my bags of gear. I got busy crawling around up there from rafter to rafter, rigging everything.

I had three cameras fitted with wide-angle lenses and time-lapse motor drives and add-on loads of fast film. Each one would take 250 shots at whatever intervals I set. I used duct tape to fasten one camera to the end rafter in the corner, aiming the lens down at an angle so the field of view took in the whole floor of the barn. I placed the second camera catty-corner, taped to a rafter at the back of the barn and aimed it to take in the same field from the opposite angle. I taped the third camera to the middle of the middle rafter and aimed it straight down, so I wound up with three overhead angles on anything that happened below. I set the remote timers to snap a shot every fifteen seconds, in a stagger, one camera starting at five, another at ten, the third at fifteen seconds after I hit the trip button, which was a little thing the size of a disposable cigarette lighter that I put in my pocket. I tested each camera for a couple of shots and rechecked the alignments and then dropped off the rafters.

Rissler had found the fuse box and he turned on the power. The yellow lights came on, hanging low under the rafters, and I walked around and checked that the cameras couldn't be spotted from down below. I swung back into the rafters, crawled around and checked everything again, and set the f-stops for the available light. Then I had a thought, about the Judge deciding to work with only one or two of the fixtures on. Maybe he was shy, and liked to do his rough-ups in lower light. I had Rissler smash out the bulbs in one of the fixtures, and then another, while I checked the light readings; then I dropped down beside him. There was only one fixture of lights still on, and unless the Judge wanted to work in the dark or by flashlight, which I doubted, that was the right light for the shooting. Once I pressed the button in my pocket, one or another of those cameras would be taking a shot every five seconds for close to an hour. Theoretically.

I was sweating from the heat up in those rafters and the hurry combined with the wait. It seemed like I'd been sweating nonstop for months. I was dusty and had splinters and drymouth. One of those motor drives was pretty old and might conk out, but if it did I had the other two as backups. The drives were designed to be silent, for shooting wild animals and other things that spooked easily, and maybe they'd be quiet enough. I had everything covered as long as I arranged to get beaten up in the barn and not outside, and not too badly or for more than an hour. I'd have to make sure of that. It was going to be a little tricky, and then tricky afterward explaining how I happened to have all these cameras rigged when I was just happening to get beaten up. I couldn't exactly admit I had sicced the Judge on myself, but I thought I had that covered too. I had come down to rig these cameras to shoot another dogfight that was scheduled for next week. I wanted to get some new angles on the dogs, and the Judge had happened by and jumped to the whole thing and taken it out on me, bad luck.

Rissler had his role. He had come along as my hard-hitting, hands-on editor, but would cleverly hide out once the Judge showed up. Then he would get to trigger a rescue. He was going to use my walkie-talkie — all the shooters at the paper carried them — to hail the nearest sheriff's substa-tion and report a particular beating in progress that de-manded immediate attention. I had Rissler and the deputies as insurance and I had backups on the equipment; really, there was going to be nothing to it. The Judge and his boys and I were just going to do this Arizona dance that might get me the Pulitzer. That was how I had it figured.

Rissler had to pretend to make a final check of everything. He'd been very much the commander of this little mission, tersely asking me if I had this or that rigged right when he had no idea if I did, glancing at his watch, ducking outside too many times to watch for the Judge. He peered up toward each of the cameras, inspected around in the straw and dust on the floor for any clue we might have left. He picked up the jagged base of a broken light bulb and that gave him the chance to really contribute.

"Better not leave this lying here. Don't want them goug-ing you with it." He threw the bulb down to the far end of the barn, where it finished shattering. "You think he'll come?"

"I don't know."

"He'll come." Rissler clicked the walkie-talkie on and off, on and off, making static. "Well, I better find a spot outside.

Don't want him catching both of us in here." He tried out a
tough smile that he almost got away with. "Macky . . ."

"Yeah. What is it?"

"This is still crazy. Really fucking crazy."

"So? Arizona is crazy. It's the coyotes howling, or everybody breathing smelter smoke, or bad tequila or the effect of
all those javelina droppings, or just that Arizona sun sizzling
off brain cells. Everybody's crazy here."

He held out his hand, and I had to give him five.

He went out the door. I was all by myself under the yellow
light. I had another camera around my neck as a decoy, so
nobody would go looking for the cameras that really mattered. I clicked off some shots of the empty dog ring.

They came a half hour before midnight and didn't care if I
heard them. It sounded like the big pickup they used for
ranch chores. Their engine shut off and doors slammed, and
then it was quiet. The Judge strolled in the barn door. He had
the pit bull Devil on a leash. Behind him was Big Ed
Dempsey blinking his sick milky eyes. The three of them
closed in on me. I pushed the button to start the cameras up
in the rafters. I thought I could hear some faint clicking up
there, and then thought I couldn't. Larry the Rat popped in a
little door behind me and called out, "Clear back here."

The Judge said, "Scout around for anything that doesn't
look right." Larry the Rat ducked out. "I shouldn't be here.
I really shouldn't." He lit a cigarillo and stared at the door
where L.R. had disappeared. "There's a place I go, down on
the coast in Mexico, that gets a breeze this time of year. It
comes off the salt water and rustles the palm trees. You can
get a genuine thatched hut with your own hammock right on
the sand. Even now not many people know about it. It's
never crowded. The people there dress in white and are glad

to have you down. Every afternoon it rains for twenty minutes and cleans everything off and at night the waves are like a massage. It's been too long since I've been down there."

Larry the Rat came in the back door. "Looks okay."

The Judge looked at me. "Tell me your name again."

I aimed the camera around my neck at him and Devil and took a picture. I took another one of Big Ed, who started for me, but the Judge motioned him off. "Wait a minute or two."

"It's Macky. Of the *News-Gazette*."

"The fucking Artful Dodger," Big Ed said.

I took another picture of him.

"A lousy snapshot artist," the Judge said. "Roy's quick snaps. That part of what you told me was true. The rest was lies. Every bit of the rest of it. You came into my house and tricked me out of whiskey and food and information about dogfighting."

"Send me a bill for the refreshments. The paper'll be good for it."

"And now here we are. I have to respond. It's become a matter of honor. Of principle. There was a time when I might have let it slide. But when a man gets as old as I am, he finds himself more free to do the right thing."

"So cancel your subscription."

"I'll cancel *you*." He jabbed the cigarillo at me, red-faced. He drew it back, smoked it. "How do you see this, Macky, some big exposé? About people letting their dogs fight? Letting their dogs do what dogs want to do? What they must do? You think this is a big deal? I suppose you can make it look like one. You can make it look like anything. Nobody likes you for it. Nobody at all. How do you think I got onto you? Somebody you've fucked over, it doesn't matter how, in your line of work you learn to do it without thinking and it carries over to everything you do. I've seen journalists. I had to deal with them for years on the bench. They aren't that much worse than anyone else except they're so damn proud of it. What do you have on me, Macky? Some pictures of my dogs? You haven't got much, not yet, or you wouldn't be down here fooling around. Whatever paltry evidence you've managed to put together, it's going to come down to my word against yours, my reputation against yours, and most people not caring either way. It'd be interesting to see who'd come out on top in that match. Maybe there won't even be any story except one about what's going to happen here tonight."

"The paper knows what I'm up to."

"And you think your ass is covered? Nobody's ass is covered. Not totally. Not if somebody else wants it badly enough. Fuck the paper. Nobody who isn't here right now is going to affect this. I could accidentally lose my grip on this leash and before any of us could stop him Devil would be grinding into you." He flicked the leash and Devil lunged against it, straining to get me, making no noise. "It wouldn't be anyone's doing, just an accident. If there was any blame it'd be on poor Devil. He's just a victim of breeding. He might rip your throat out or cripple you for life. We might have to kill him to get him off of you. They'd kill him later anyhow. Give him the gas or the injection. I don't want to lose Devil. He'd be hard to replace. But this is the sort of thing that can happen." The Judge flicked the leash again, like he was about to let go, but it was a signal to Devil to sit.

"There are tried-and-true methods. You could just get lost. Fall down a mine shaft and never be found. You could have a smash-up in your car. You could commit suicide. Hanging, pills. I'd say you're the blow-your-brains-out type. That interest you, Macky? Would that look believable? We'd have alibis. Nothing could be proved beyond a reasonable doubt. It's a high standard. I know the law."

Larry the Rat laughed.

"You contemplate how far I'm going to take it," the Judge said. "Hit him a few times, Ed."

Big Ed tugged on worn leather work gloves. Larry the Rat clamped my arms from behind and I put up a little struggle. I let him confiscate my decoy camera — I didn't want to get into a tug of war. I wanted to act valiant but dignified while I got beat up on the record. Big Ed moved in and I thought it would be a nice touch to try kicking him. He slapped it aside and swung down and slammed me with a fist. He slammed me again and then I lost track. I was on my hands and knees spitting blood. Something smashed on a concrete slab next to me. Larry the Rat had my camera by the strap and was whipping it on the slab. He smashed it open and tore out the film and pawed through my camera bag. I got up dizzy. Big Ed loomed under the yellow lights. I tried not to grin, and then went ahead anyway. They wouldn't be able to figure it out.

"You took advantage of me," the Judge said. "But what's unpardonable is how you used Alice."

"You treat her so well."

"I understand her. She could go off the deep end over this. She could turn on all of us. She'd be better off if she never saw you again. We'd all be better off. The world would be . . . Some more, Ed."

Big Ed moved in and hit me. I collapsed and rolled and he was kicking me. He backed off and I lay there. I tried to get up and fell down. I sat with my back against a pole and concentrated on breathing. I couldn't get a full breath.

The Judge squatted down next to me. "I'm not doing this for you or for me. I'm doing it for Alice."

He had them haul me to my feet and start on me again. The barn rocked around me and I went down again. I was having a hard time thinking about anything. I had a sick smile on my face. Somebody hauled me up far enough to shove my head in a bucket of water. I breathed in water and choked and fought them. They shoved me into the bucket again. Everything was going great. Those cameras up in the rafters must have been getting some terrific shots. My story was really coming together. Except for the little fact that they were killing me.

14

WITH MY WORLD reduced to the insides of a nine-ninety-nine bucket, the confining metal was a gray blur scraping my face and ears and skull as I thrashed to get out, the water sealing me under with noises from a madhouse: the close impacts transmitting through bone, the bucket scraping along the floor, the sloshing and cursing and grunts of exertion. I went wild whipping my body against them and they grabbed my hair, twisting it to the roots, and forced me to kneel and held me under.

Don't scream, don't swallow, the water burns, blast off on the pain and the foaming pink blood and puke. Get a leg free and then an arm to knock over the bucket and suck in chunks of air. Slopping under them on the slick boards, focus the panic, wriggle, do anything to get loose, fuck dignity, they've captured the leg again and no, bastards, leave the arm free, isn't this enough? — gagging, coughing, dizzy with lungs shivering — the stream from the spigot churning down, refilling the bucket — can't suck in enough of this air that's dirty with straw and blood, somebody should say something, not just the bucket! Suck in and here goes, you wanted it Macky you got it, into the bucket again and now you're back to running the Arizona rapids.

My guts curdled and soured. Powerless, I wrenched against their holds. Sagging, going limp — they didn't fall for it. I had to scream now. Gag and scream, lungs seized on empty. My teeth clicking against the metal, biting frantically and uselessly. My asshole puckered and between my legs tingled. One last shot to let them have it with everything. *Rock and roll.* Then I was flat on my back gazing up at the yellow light that was swinging like a demented pendulum — shadow, glare, shadow, glare. As Big Ed's shadow swayed over me and brought me back, I doubled up coughing blood and water, puked violently, the bile stinging the cuts on my lips. I wallowed in my filth and tried to focus. What are they looking at? The open barn door where a man was waving his arms. Only then did I hear Rissler shouting.

"That's all! That's all!"

"Hell," the Judge muttered. He dropped the bucket.

Big Ed's shadow moved off me. He stepped toward Rissler as I slaved to get up, all unconnected, hauling each breath. The floor swaying with the yellow light. Big Ed owned the long moment, lumbering toward his target. He bore down and Rissler yelled —

"Press!"

— Big Ed swatted aside the brandished card and hit him, a tremendous backhand slap on the jaw that cracked across the barn. Rissler's head snapped sideways and he suspended on the impact and in slow motion crumpled.

"Oh-oh," Larry the Rat singsonged.

The Judge jabbed his fingers through his wet hair, making an ugly grimace.

I staggered for the back door. The latch was a rope pull that stuck and then gave. Outside the ground dropped; my balance was bad, my wet clothes dragged. The door thumped against the barn behind me and I heard them

trading orders. In the dark and the shape I was in I couldn't
see anything except the bouncing stars and just ran against
the raw pain in my chest, across the ruts and down the gentle
slope, my thoughts consumed by pumping lungs and a red
vision of Devil in the ring. Tree hulks reared up and clawed at
me with their thorns. In among the mesquites anything
could have been hiding, I had to stop, bend over and try to
suck in full breaths that would never be anything but raw and
sour and listen to my blood pounding and then Devil's collar
clinking, coming for me. He was out there panting. I ran,
crashed into a nightmare and fell in a clutter of branches,
fought the hideous texture of it, the hollow bones and beating wings and hooking talons and beak: a huge flat-faced
owl, shrieking and flapping and struggling out from under
me, swooping off crookedly. I was laughing madly now and
sliding down into a rocky wash that had runoff from the rains,
splashing down the wash with noises too close behind me,
sprawling against a bank. I banged up the slope and into my
car and scratched my way inside. Digging in my soggy
pocket for the key. *Wham* against the side window — Devil!

Yeah, here he is with the teeth, Macky, look down his
bore isn't he pretty as he tries to tear off the door handle and
eat through the glass, suck it up one more time and pick
yourself up off the seat. Don't ask why the glass is still
holding, thread that key into the ignition right the fuck now,
and of course the car doesn't want to start, why should it?

The window on the passenger side shattered and Big Ed
lunged in. The car started, I stomped the gas and his big
hands receded, grabbed onto the door. He ran, dragged,
dropped off as the big pickup raced in from the right and
tried to ram me. I swerved hard and careened down into the
wash, tires spinning and burning until the engine died.
Stuck. I crawled out on top of the car and took my belt off and

tried a couple of lashes against the fender and waited for
Devil. A man with a flashlight hiked down the bank and lit
me up. "Drop it."

"Says who?"

"Pima County Sheriff's Department."

The Judge was holding court on a hay bale in the barn,
with Devil on the leash. One of the deputies had to be an old
pal of his.

"Hello, Dave," the Judge said.

"What's this all about?"

"It'll be hell sorting it out."

The other deputy bent over something by the door. "This
one's dead."

"His neck seems to be broken," the Judge said.

I kneeled by the body. "Shit, Rissler."

"Who is he?"

My fingers curled into Rissler's shirt, made fists. "He's a
journalist. He's the editor of the fucking year."

"Hey, buddy. You look pretty beat up."

"Get away from me."

Big Ed stood over us. "A lovely corpse. Old Charlie
Dickens had this right too. I killed him. Going blind and to
prison." He took a heavy step away from us and another and
then started jogging like he was in no great hurry or didn't
know where to go or want to get there. They yelled for him to
stop but he didn't. When he was almost beyond the range of
the headlights of their patrol truck in the yard he whirled and
aimed his big hand and yelled "*Bam!*" and they shot him
twice.

"Christ."

"He was faking it."

"I swear he had a gun."

A wind blew through me, harder and louder. I had to shout over it. "Rissler. Rissler." I don't know what I was shouting. Faceless shadows were holding me again. I fought them and the wind and the blackness.

I came to the next day in the hospital. They had me in clean white sheets. They didn't know. I was wearing bandages and an i.v. I could look out a window at the sky, which looked blue and hot. If you've never seen the sky in Arizona you might not believe that. I was sore all over, sorer in specific places. A nurse came in with the happy routine and I was nasty to her. Then a doctor who wasn't happy at all told me I had a broken rib and other lesser things wrong with me, but I was going to be all right. He didn't seem to care either way, and that was all right too. Everything was all right and that was the hell of it. I thought maybe I'd just stay in that room for the next couple of years. But there were people who wanted me and some of them were waiting outside making a commotion and they wouldn't wait long. I had a little time to get the facts.

The papers were on the nightstand. We hadn't made deadline for the *News-Gazette* but the afternoon daily had the story on page one. The *Evening Error*, we used to call it, neck-and-neck competition for our own *Morning Mistake*. In sixty-point bold the headline across the *Evening Error* announced, EDITOR KILLED IN LATE-NIGHT BRAWL. Of course there hadn't been any brawl, and there were a half-dozen other errors in the first few graphs, but it wasn't any worse than most of what you read. They had a file photo of Rissler looking respectable like he never did in a suitcoat and knotted tie, and an old shot of the Judge looking even more respectable in his courtroom robes. The readers would be diving into the story to find out how two such community pillars got mired in shit. The story didn't deliver much after that, there were more holes than facts. They had it up high, how Rissler and I had been investigating pit-bull fights, somebody at the *Morning Mistake* had let out that much, but they didn't have anything more on that angle. The Judge was no commenting all over the place, and so was the sheriff's department, except to report that Rissler had apparently been killed by a blow to the face, and the man who apparently killed him had then apparently been killed by the deputies. Inside they had a head shot that looked something like me, and a driver's license mug of the late Big Ed. Then they went to the unnamed sources: Sources said, the Judge did indeed raise pit bulls but was steadfastly opposed to fighting them, and had heard this old barn was being used for fights, and had gone down there to check it out, and had run up against two pushy journalists not, incidentally, employed by the *Evening Error*, who apparently made accusations and apparently started a rumble. Sources said. Which meant the Judge or one of his cronies in the sheriff's department or prosecutor's office had leaked it out. The *Evening Error* had been glad to go with it because it looked bad for the *Morning Mistake*.

The door swung open and I tossed the papers on the floor. Ganged up in the hallway outside were journalists from the papers and eyewitness TV crews and even some poor bastards from radio. You get that many in the middle of the day, when there isn't much going on. They get so desperate for news they run out for a story on a chicken getting loose. Now they all wanted to eyewitness me.

A plainclothes sheriff's man held the door so I could see. He came inside and closed it, a little amused smile on his face. He was one I knew: J. D. Foster, with a face like a fist, the type that thinks not letting you know his first name gives him an edge. He'd gotten as far as captain with it.

"Give me your version," he said. "We'll match it up to the facts and see what we got."

Of course I wasn't too popular with the department. I'd done some nailing of cop-types over the years, capped off by the usual package on police brutality, shots of ravaged suspects and so-called innocent bystanders who'd also gotten it. They hadn't liked that at headquarters. To the cops no one is innocent, only uncaught. Not that they're far off, but they refuse to consider themselves anywhere among the guilty.

I told J. D. Foster, "I've got a lot to say and it'll match up with the facts. But first I talk to the paper. I was on a job for them and they have to know how it came out."

"What kind of job?"

"My head hurts."

"Then we'll keep you in custody until it stops hurting. You're a material witness to somebody getting killed."

"Maybe I am. Maybe I'm not. My head hurts so much I can't remember right now. Send in somebody from the paper and maybe I'll feel better and remember. Otherwise it'll bring out our lawyers."

The L-word did it. "Who do you want?"

"I saw Burke out there."

J. D. Foster went out and brought in Skippy Burke. "It's too crowded in here," I said. "My head."

"I'm glad," J. D. Foster said. But he took the hint, and left.

Of course Burke had on a black armband. And I had to make him explain it. "What's that?"

"What d'you think? It's for Rissler."

"I suppose they passed them out in the newsroom. Your idea?"

"Yes."

"And everybody who couldn't stand him put one on."

"He's dead, Macky."

"Nobody has as many pals as a dead man."

"You're acting like it was your fault. Was it?"

"No," I said. "No, it wasn't."

"Then you better work on your delivery."

Burke was pretty sharp. And now he had opportunity. He'd been Rissler's second-in-command, the assistant managing editor, a golden boy ascending fast until he ran into Rissler and got relegated to the journalistic equivalent of mopping floors and wiping out ashtrays. He'd been assigned the job of overseeing city desk on daily coverage, while Rissler kept for himself all the special projects and anything that looked hot. Burke had toiled away for years making sure the coverage of all the school-board elections was balanced and everybody's name was spelled right in the paper and nobody on cityside was taking too much overtime or lunches that ran twelve minutes too long, and now he was a middle-aged golden boy with a fat neck, still trying to get everybody to call him Skippy, only now nobody would. We're all shaped by our jobs and Burke had wound up a stickler for details that nobody else cared about. He dressed every day in gray or off-gray suits with matching vests buttoned all the way up, and nondescript ties. He had all his hair and kept it trimmed and parted neatly. He shaved every day and he never smiled too widely or frowned too deeply or laughed too loud. He did everything within certain parameters, and was sharp enough to see what he had given up. Now that Rissler was out of the way I had no doubt that Burke was going to make people pay.

"You never were too good on organization," Burke said. "I'm acting M.E. now. I'm running the newsroom. Sorry, but this is business. Any confession you want to make, make it to me."

Because I needed the paper's backing more than ever, I

confessed all right — but not to everything. I went over my
investigation of the Judge and his dogfighting, and how Rissler got killed. I edited out some of Alice Malone, and all
mention of how Rissler would still be alive if we hadn't lured
the Judge into on-the-record violence. Burke was enough of a
newsman to get excited about the story. He wasn't as obvious
as Rissler, he just pinched his shirt cuffs and worked a finger
inside his watchband. For Burke, that was getting carried
away.

"Send somebody down to that barn to get those cameras I
planted in the rafters," I told him. "The sheriff probably has
the scene taped off or something, but I doubt anyone'll be
around. Just get in however you can. Whatever you do, don't
turn the film over to the sheriff. Later on we can make copies
of some prints and turn them over. Right now they'd tie
everything up in court and it'd be public record and everyone
could use it. This is still my story."

"Our story. You aren't working alone."

"We'll do this right for Rissler, if you want to think of it
like that, or if you have to tell anyone higher up. And for the
paper's name. Get a lawyer down here to spring me and I'll
come in and run the film myself. I'll have to write something
to go with whatever shots we use. We might as well run the
whole package right now while we've got everybody's attention."

Burke didn't like me giving so many orders, but he saw
they were right on, and he got behind the story. "We'll have
to hustle. I'll push back deadline to midnight. We'll go with
all the dogfight shots, everything. Okay, Macky. Let's hope
those cameras at the barn got enough to clear you. We're in
serious jeopardy on this one."

He went out and the sheriff's man came back in and I told
him a leaner version of the story, minus, of course, mention of

the cameras that had to be retrieved and the photos we already had. He brought in a couple more from the department and they taped me telling it again. They didn't want to believe me at first, but the worse it looked for the Judge the better they liked it. They were no different from anyone else. They liked to bring the big ones down. They wanted proof about the dogfighting and the killing and I told them I might be able to provide some. That was a mistake, because they jumped all over me. I told them I just meant I'd do some more digging and I had some ideas. They said I'd have to testify and I said I knew that. By then we were getting along fine. A lawyer from the paper showed up — Cass Unger, pale and keg-shaped in a gray skirt-suit. She had a reputation for snorting coke and arguing guilty guys off death row, and it didn't take much for her to get them to let me go. I got dressed in my beaten-up clothes and slipped on a black armband that Burke had left me, one of his details. I went into the hallway and shoved through the gang of journalists who bombarded me with the wrong questions. I wasn't answering anyway. The sheriff's men didn't help me hold them off. I got outside and into the lawyer's car and she drove me down to the paper without asking any questions at all.

I let her march into the building ahead of me. I folded over, braced against the trunk of the car, fixing my eyes on the horizon of oil-stained asphalt between my shoes. Straightened up to catch the sun glinting off the razor wire that was coiled along the top of the fence surrounding me and the parking lot. I went inside, up to the newsroom, and they had the cameras and had developed the negatives from the fight that had killed Rissler and was going to make me a hero. The negs looked good. Everything looked far too good.

15

WE HAD A BIG MEETING and then an even bigger one with everyone at the paper who wanted to get in on it. We broke into smaller meetings, and then had another big one. In between we got some work done, gathering together all the shots from the dogfights and the dog training and some atmospheric stuff from the Judge's house that Rissler had been keeping locked in his office. We picked out the best shots and argued over our favorites and proved that everybody sees things differently. Burke made the final decisions, going along with me on almost everything except for a few that he had to have his own way on, so everybody would understand how critically important his new role was.

"What's wrong with this one?" Burke asked.

"That woman there on the left is Alice Malone. We promised to keep her out of it as much as possible."

"What else did we promise her? It's a good shot. Look at the crowd."

"We've got other ones that work as well and don't show her. Look at this."

Then we had to hassle over the last batch of shots, which showed me getting beaten up and Rissler getting killed.

"God, Macky, they really laid into you."

"Ouch."

"You need a little work on that spin kick."

I had to put up with a certain amount of petty harassment but pretty quick we got down to which photos would reproduce the best on newsprint and tell the story with the most impact. They made a good study of humanity, looking down in dim light on two men hitting and kicking another while a fourth one watched and smoked his cigarillos.

"I like these of Macky getting his head shoved in the water bucket."

"We won't use these."

"Why not, Macky? You don't want a hundred and fifty thousand shots of you wearing a bucket going all over town?"

"They tell the story," Burke said. "We'll use them."

There was a lot we were ignoring or handling with black humor until the story got done, to protect ourselves from other emotions, and because we were journalists and this is what journalists do.

"This is a nice one-two-three sequence of the big guy swatting Rissler."

"There he goes into journalist's heaven."

"Think he made it?"

"He's got as good a chance as anybody. Where the news-hole is bottomless and the expense money comes without question and a story can take as long as it takes."

We laughed, and then it caught up to us, and we had an uncomfortable moment of silence for Rissler, one of several we had for him, whenever the tension cut through or we couldn't think of anything to say. We dedicated the special section to him and ran his file photo in a little box in the upper-right-hand corner of the cover, which was a huge blow-up of a dogfight. There was a black-line border all the way around that I thought was a little too heavy, but it was Burke's idea. Burke ran his line around the inside pages too, where we laid out the other photos and some copy I tapped out on a terminal, sparse copy as we didn't want to bother the readers with much reading. We put in the names of the other dog-fighters we were sure of, and didn't identify those we weren't, and talked about how we would follow up and nail as many as we could. We had the lawyers look at everything and then told them to go to hell. And of course we argued about a catchy title and a logo for the package, and Max Durazo wanted *Dog Eat Dog*, and Doris from promotion wanted *Deadly Sport*, which got some support until Burke rewrote it into *Death in the Ring*, which nobody liked. Finally we couldn't spend any more time on it and settled on *Dogfight*.

We had momentum: The closer we got to deadline the faster everybody and everything went. It was the journalism combine at its finest. At five o'clock and then again at ten we broke to check out what TV was doing with it, flicking around on the sets in the newsroom. All the stations led with the story, their lopped-off, slanted versions of it.

"They're all going with the handout from the sheriff."

"Listen to that grammar."

"They aren't chasing the Judge. Not until somebody hands them some real ammo."

"We'll hand them plenty tomorrow morning. They're just building demand for us. We got the story and they'll all have to come to us."

We only missed the pushed-back deadline by ten minutes, and even Burke wasn't counting up what the overtime would come to, or if he was, he was doing it silently. We would have staged a real newsroom celebration, with the usual back-slapping, if we could have forgotten about why Rissler wasn't there. But we had on those damn black arm-bands, so we couldn't.

A bottle of whiskey or two got dredged up out of bottom drawers, which almost restored my faith in the news business. It was a solemn celebration, warm whiskey in coffee cups, not much being said, and it turned into one large and stretching moment of silence for Rissler. Not that we'd all been his buddies. But he'd been filling the newsroom with himself for years and now the biggest story was that he was gone. The copy was headed down to the press room, and we were a bunch of people after midnight. One of us had died. We had to face that fact, and the whiskey, under the fluorescent lights.

The worst was when Suzy Kino decided to give me a neck rub. She got behind me — "Relax, Macky" — and burrowed her fingers into me. "We all miss him. Who's this Alice Malone?"

"Somebody in a photograph, that's all."

"That's a no comment if I ever heard one." She used her fingers on me. "You're all tightened up. I hope she's treating you right. Or should I say, wrong."

After a while Max Durazo made a crack about Burke, who had already moved into Rissler's office and was using Rissler's phone to check on the press run. That loosened things up for other cracks about who would therefore move into Burke's office, and the jockeying for position Rissler's death would cause all the way down the ranks. Maybe it sounds a little ruthless, but this is how it works. On a newspaper everybody is waiting for everybody else to stumble and go down in front of the combine. Rissler had gone down, and it was too bad, but it made for opportunity and of course resentment against anyone who moved up. Gossiping about it was another way to not think directly about Rissler — how his head snapped, and the broken angle of his neck in the photos we'd been studying all day.

I had reams to not think about: How Big Ed looked in the last of the photos starting his run toward the barn door and nowhere. How I ached down to my little hairs from the beating. How Alice for some reason wasn't answering the phone at my place. How Rissler and I had set it all up. And how the shakes were simmering inside me, ready to erupt any second and betray me.

Before I could get out of there I had to deal with Burke. He called me into his new office and was very much the man behind the desk.

"This whole story depends on you, Macky. The paper and the staff, the credibility of all of us comes down to you. I'm not pleased about it. I have to live with decisions you and Rissler made. I might have to correct some. If this story goes over well, if your version holds up, I'll back you like Rissler did. At least as long as the story lasts. Then we might have to reassess. Because the methods you and Rissler used aren't mine. I'm going to instill discipline on this paper, and ethics. And I'm going to emphasize the positive side of the news. We've been focusing too much on the negative. I'm going to have at least one bit of good news on the front page every day. I want people smiling when they read this paper."

"They smile now. They'll be smiling tomorrow morning."

"Not that way. That's not what I mean. You and Rissler had them smiling like buzzards."

"Or like realists."

"Any word you want. Realism is on the way out. People are burned out by it. It's unpleasant."

"That's what the surveys show?"

"Some of them. I know this is a bad time but we're in a fast-moving business and I have to say, we can publish this paper without you, Macky."

"Why don't we call back the dogfight package and draw

smile buttons in the margins? We can pin one on Rissler's shirt at the funeral."

"There's a section in the employees manual about insubordination. Read it. I'm professionalizing this operation. If you want to last you'll keep that in mind."

"We wouldn't want to speak too freely, would we? Not in the communication business."

That got him. He smacked the desk and jumped up and glared at me. Then he sat back down. That was Burke.

"You've been sniping at me all day," he said. "I don't like what happened to Rissler. It's not my fault. I asked you once, was it yours? Is that why you're acting like this? This newspaper is not going soft. We're going after the Judge and the other dogfighters and anybody who had anything to do with killing Rissler. If you had anything to do with it, more than what you've told me already, if you've acted unprofessionally, I'll come after you with every resource this paper has. Your story better hold up."

"Good news. It will."

"Let's have a drink to Rissler."

I stood and bided my time. The little sounds and motions amplified as he broke open the seal on the bottle he must've bought on the way in that morning and poured out a couple of whiskeys. Of course his went into the official glass that was glorified with the decal of the *News-Gazette* masthead. He swallowed, I swallowed. He watched me over the rim of his official glass. I concentrated on my hands squeezing my glass, the ripples ricocheting around the rationed inch of amber whiskey. Only a few little tremors.

I left and drove to my place churning about Burke and his ethics. Ethics are the latest thing in journalism, the subject of endless conferences and speeches and browbeating about exactly when not to go undercover, use hidden tape recorders or cameras, get close to sources or go with anything that is off the record or at all impolite. Ethics are killing journalism, with more and more journalists concentrating on why they shouldn't get a real story instead of why they should, and if it keeps on, there will only be ethical journalists with ethical stories that say and accomplish nothing. It's hard enough to nail anybody with all the intimidation and lying and cover-ups that are handed out, without having to invent ways to make it harder. If you always had to be one hundred percent square, maybe you could nail somebody once in a great while, by interviewing half the population and digging through truckloads of documents and then getting lucky, but there is no time for that with the combine on your back. Journalists like to pack up, and now they are packing up around ethics and making a profession out of it; that explained Burke. He was driving the journalism combine now, the one that was bearing down on me. Ethics. They are just another excuse for journalists to go after other journalists, which is what we love the most.

Alice was my immediate ethics problem — a source I'd gotten too close to, as they say. You can guess how I felt when I got to my place and found her doing the tarantula routine. She was kneeling on my concrete porch, reaching into the flower bed that was mostly shriveled flowers and weeds and dirt. The porch light was on. There was a big tarantula crawling around back in there. She flattened her hand on the dirt in front of it.

"Watch this," she said.

The tarantula crawled onto her hand. Slowly she raised it, keeping her fingers stiff, and stood up and showed me the hairy thing, thick black legs and hard-shell body and preda-

tory eyes. It's another pride of Arizona, spiders as big as
kittens. Dozens to the acre living in holes in the ground.
Summer nights they crawl out of their holes and go searching
for mates, all these horny tarantulas, and they turn up crossing the roads, or clinging to screen doors. They were primitive enough for me. Leg by leg the tarantula crawled off her
hand and started up her bare arm.

"They can't tell you from a log," she said. "They won't
bite unless you scare them."

"I'm home from the office, Alice."

"Then you should kiss me, dear. Watch out for my tarantula." She eased her arm out to the side with the spider. She
had on her black outfit, the band top and miniskirt, and she
was barefoot. I didn't move and she came into me and kissed
me. The tarantula crawled up to her shoulder.

"Take it, Macky."

I touched her shoulder and let the tarantula crawl on my
hand with its legs scratching me lightly and gave it a ride
down to the dirt.

"My man," Alice said. She wrapped herself around me.
"Am I too weird for you? Is this too weird?" She rubbed my
hand on parts of her. "I think your tolerance for weirdness is
high. I played your answering machine. You didn't erase it.
The tape you made to lure the Judge into action. I put it away
somewhere. I won't tell anyone if you do what I say. I'm glad
you did it, Macky. Can I show you how glad? Feel this. And
this."

I swept by her and went inside. The little cassette was
missing. I dumped out the drawer where she'd moved in her
things, made a mess searching the closet, flipping off the
couch cushions and the mattress, tumbling books off shelves.

"Maybe I have it on me," she said.

I slapped her chest and tore her top off over her head. She

slid against the wall and covered herself with her arms and
looked shocked and afraid. That was a first. It stopped me for
a moment and then her eyes glittered and I grabbed her
shoulders and started shaking her.

"Where is it? Where is it?"

She was smiling as her spittle flew. She must've bit her lips
or tongue because she started bleeding again. I didn't want
any more visions of blood. I let her go and she danced around
me, slid down and hugged my thighs and struggled to open
my fly with her tongue and teeth.

I pried back her head. Her mouth had left bloodstains on
my pants.

"It's too bad they didn't shoot him."

She was lying against me in bed, and for a moment I
thought she meant Rissler, then I got it: She was still after the
Judge. The cooler was on low and all I could do was sweat,
and stare at the ceiling and the corners of the room closing in.

16

THE *DOGFIGHT* PACKAGE didn't give us
any peace. It hit the streets and before seven A.M.
the phone was ringing and the early-bird eyewitness TV
crews had us under siege and the law was banging on the
door. I told Alice to stay out of sight and not answer the phone
or talk to anybody and then went out into it. The ones in
charge took me downtown where a battery from the sheriff's
department and the county prosecutor had me go over my
version of everything again and then finally they got around
to what they really wanted, which was all the negatives and
prints that showed dogfights or Rissler getting killed. By then
the lawyers from the paper caught up and our lawyers went
around with their lawyers and various amendments to the
constitution got invoked and trampled upon and reinvoked,
and then their lawyers got tired of it and put me in jail. That
was all right, it was just a holding cell in the courthouse, and I
had it all to myself; none of the lawyers could get to me in
there. But after a couple of hours our lawyers argued me out in
a hearing in which I got to act valiant and stand tall and say
nothing about the deal that had been made: I had to give
them prints of everything, we got to keep the negs, and
anything they handed out to other media, we had to get

credit. Half the journalists in Arizona were all over the courthouse and I got to tell them nothing too, even though they
were all shouting for Macky to come on and give each one and
not the other the inside dope. They ganged me out to the
courthouse steps, where of course we ran into the Judge.

He was marching up the steps with somebody who had to
be his lawyer, and another hack from the prosecutor's office.
He stopped and stared at me and I stared back. The cameras
were going and journalists were popping questions all around
us, but it was just him and me. He threw back his head and
laughed, the way he had that day Alice and I found him
holding session in his swimming pool, whiskeyed and
sunburned — only this time he was loud. He laughed and
wound it down and shook his head, and went on up the steps.
It was going to make a good snippet on the evening news.

Rissler's death made the story even bigger than we'd
planned. Once the Judge was charged with accessory to
second-degree murder, along with dogfighting and some
other crimes connected with me getting worked over, the
wires and big out-of-state papers got on it; so did the TV
networks. They stayed on it for weeks. My *Dogfight* package
made every front page and special segment and then the
national mags. I wanted to hide but Burke got the idea of me
having a press conference, and I had to face them all and go
through everything again and then pull up my shirt to show
off my bruises and the bandage over my broken rib. Shots of
that circulated a little too widely too. Out of all of them only
a couple pressed me on the real question, about how I just
happened to have my cameras set up in the perfect position
to record my beating and Rissler's murder, but I handled it.
They were journalists looking for an angle nobody else had,
so I got each one alone and fed them.

"Big Ed wasn't all bad. He went around quoting Charlie Dickens. Yeah, I'm not kidding."

"The rattlesnake-skin couch? Didn't I mention that before?"

That took their minds off me and sent the journalism combine rumbling in another direction.

Then one afternoon I had to go out under the sun and say good-bye to Rissler. It was another intimate occasion attended by hundreds of journalists from all over, only this time some of them weren't just providing coverage. There was a field of lush green grass — nowhere does a cemetery look as inviting as in Arizona — and even a few trees throwing shade. The shade didn't reach Rissler's grave. They had a generic minister, one Rissler might have tolerated, talk about the final deadline nobody misses. Rissler's sister from Cleveland broke down, and we had to sweat through Burke reading the editorial eulogy from that morning's edition. Then it was my turn. I'd had plenty of warning, but I wasn't ready.

"He — "

I coughed the spiders out of my throat.

"He was a man who lived and died for the story. He wanted to get it all down in words and pictures. This is what happens in the business. Give me five, Rissler," and I slapped the casket, and again on the upswing.

A hot wind whisked off the desert as they lowered his casket out of the bright sunlight into the hole. In a cloud of dust they started covering him up.

The story gained momentum. Journalism mags called me up to do stories on how my story had been done, and to discuss what they called the issues. A couple of graduate students from the big journalism schools wanted to include me in their theses. I got invited to speak at a conference that was coming up in town, on the relationship between journalism and society. The paper was putting me up for the Pulitzer and every other journalism award. Letters of recommendation and more invitations and requests for interviews were coming in from people all over who wanted to get in on it. Some of the big papers were talking jobs. I had become a story, and I couldn't stop it.

I didn't have to do much work anymore. Burke assembled a team to do the mop-up, identifying the other dogfighters and covering their busts and the progress of the cases. I'd turned into a front man, representing my story and the paper, and waiting around for the right opportunity to move on and up. Of course the others in the newsroom resented it, and that made me more isolated there than ever. I'd put in half days and then I'd go running in the heat, but it seemed like I could never run fast enough, and then I'd go home to Alice, the woman I had to keep from the world, and we'd start on each other and the tequila and I never got to sleep easily.

She had worked herself into me and with the job done we ticked off the time until we could find out why, her retreating for hours up on the flat roof at my place, absorbing the sun, burning herself darker and then coming down, hot to the touch, to give it to me good. Sometimes I'd go up there and she'd be covered all over with markings from different-colored felt-tip pens — lightning bolts and spirals and all sorts of geometry and doodling, and maybe a big smile or frown inked on her face — she was a master of surprises! — and she'd have to show me every little mark and tell me why she'd made it; then I'd take her like the savage she was. She'd fuck me to sleep and wake me up in the morning with some variation of her on all fours over me with her breasts caressing my cheeks. We'd go out in the desert, strip down and hike on through the menacing cactus needles and grit, wary of what a reckless move would mean, and when we couldn't be teased any longer we'd abandon caution and really go at it. She had me hooked in so many ways. And we were both so desperate.

With all our grasping gyrations, I sensed we were trying to heal up and reassure ourselves about what had happened — only something potent might work for us — yet even as potent as we were together, it's not physically possible to sustain the titillation. We knew something was hanging over us like an afternoon thundercloud, getting blacker. Pretty soon it was going to crash down on us, then we'd know how black it was. Then we'd know . . . What an Ozzie and Harriet we made, just another average Arizona couple shrugging at approaching doom in our home sweet. She'd play with the tarantula, which she kept in the bathtub or a shoebox or glass salad-mixing bowl. Or she'd pull out my file of Arizona worsts, and we'd thumb through the clips and play one-up giving angles the papers hadn't gotten around to covering: "Most red ants per square foot!" . . . "Most duststorms per week!" . . . "Numero uno in fundamentalist drunk drivers and hopping-mad mothers!" . . . "Where all the tap water tastes like sweat!" I had a set of the photos of Rissler getting swatted into journalist's heaven and I'd toast him with the tequila, and then again. He was another one who knew I was a simulated success.

I found out how simulated the night I gave the speech to the journalism conference. It was at one of the resort hotels, in a big hall that was full. Some of them had come a long way and were covering it as the next installment of my story. Suzy Kino was there shooting me.

"I shouldn't be up here," I told them. "For a lot of reasons. Mainly because the man who can't be here tonight is the one you really want to honor. I'm only the survivor."

Of course they tried to prove me wrong by interrupting with applause. I went on, telling them what they wanted to hear, about journalism and freedom, and journalism and truth, and journalism and democracy. The usual. I said in Arizona we can do journalism as well as anyone does anywhere. And I said we shouldn't get too proud. We should always be striving for improvement. I concluded with the little joke from William Allen White, a leading journalist from seventy years ago who most of them had never heard of: "There are three things that no one can do to the entire satisfaction of anyone else: make love, poke the fire and run a newspaper."

They loved it and I had to wait out the applause when all I wanted was a quick exit — because I could see Alice in a T-shirt dress at the back of the room. She'd come in just after I started and listened to the whole thing behind a little smile. She mixed in with the hangers-on around the podium who were congratulating me and asking what my plans were and handing me that lame rap about how they wouldn't have had the guts to do what I'd done to get those dogfight photos. She walked right up to me with that smile and the dress that was backless and she acted like we were strangers and said, "Mr. Macky, I wouldn't have had the guts either."

"You would have. It was just for the story."

She took my hand and kissed it, and one or two of them took pictures as a joke. They saw her as some journalism groupie.

"He's coming with me now," she said. She pulled my hand and backed away. They were giving me looks too. It was just like at that first dogfight and ever since — I had to go with her or make a scene. I hooked my arm through hers and we strolled toward the door, smiling and nodding good-byes.

"It would be so refreshing sometime to do something with you without the screws on."

"You like it," she said.

The perfect time to run into Burke.

"Macky. You leaving so soon?"

"Just for a few minutes."

Alice said huskily, "It might take longer."

"Your backbone looks familiar," Burke told her. "And you've got a nice way with words."

"Alice," Alice said. She shook his hand. "Alice Malone."

Burke studied her. "You aren't going to kiss mine, are you?"

"Where would that take us?"

"Does it matter?" Burke extricated his hand. "I suppose I should express the gratitude of the *News-Gazette*."

"It's already been expressed."

"I mean for the whole staff. You've done wonders for our reputation."

"That's a change for me."

"Are you seeing much of Macky?"

"Much."

"You're sort of a walking violation, aren't you?"

"Is that an invitation to lunch?"

Burke chuckled. "We could do that someday. Give me a call. We can talk about Macky."

I said, "We've got to go now and look up something in the employees manual."

"Yes," Burke said. "You look it up. And keep her in the cage."

"Bye," Alice said.

I squeezed her arm and walked her out into the landscaping away from the lights by the pool.

"What do you want, Alice?"

"I paid a visit to the sheriff's today. They had a subpoena out, wanted to ask me about some things. I read about it in the paper."

"You could've dodged them."

"I couldn't go on, never knowing when they'd pull me in." She let me dangle, then got breathless. "I told them about the dogfights. That's all. I didn't snitch you off."

I pulled her face into mine. "What's my next line?"

"I didn't!"

"What else didn't you do?"

"Your cohorts in there, all those media snots looking up to you — I didn't snitch you off to them either. Would they be shocked by the fact that you and Rissler asked for it?"

"That's their problem."

"Maybe I'll try that out on Burke at lunch. He's your new boss?"

"What do you want, Alice?"

She did her giggle. "For you to do what I say, Macky."

I shook her. "What do you want?" I had to make her say it.

"Kill him, Macky. Kill the Judge for me." Even to her the words were a strain that bulged her eyes and curled her lips. Her breath was hot. "Snuff him out. For what he did to me. Things that would make you sick. So he doesn't ever do it to anyone else."

"No! You've got to get over it without that."

"They won't send him to prison! He'll get off! They'll let him off. He's one of them and they'll find a reason. He's free right now, they let him out on bail. I read the paper. He's got his rap down, like it wasn't his fault, it was an accident and Big Ed's to blame. The lawyers'll cloud it all up. Even if they convict him they'll just give him probation or one of these honor farms. I don't care if they do send him to prison. That isn't enough, Macky."

"No."

"Murder. That's what I want. Does the word scare you, newspaperman? You won't go that far to nail somebody? You're a goddamn phony, as phony as the rest of them if you won't do it. Your ex-editor wouldn't be an ex if you'd just stayed home and played it safe, and you're carrying that around, aren't you? I'm no murderer, and neither are you, and when something happens to the Judge it won't make us murderers. We can make an exception and do it just this once. We've got reasons behind us. We'll do it together."

"No."

She broke loose and whirled and took strides for the parking lot. I got beside her. "Where are you going?"

"I can make you, Macky."

She had her pickup. I tried to stop her from getting in. She wrestled me and let out one of her little screams and people were converging on us. I had to let go of her and the remnants of any future I had went with her as she drove off. I pushed through the gapers and got to my car and chased after her, across the foothills with the city lights twinkling merrily below us, and east out into the desert. I followed her one taillight that worked, through the dips and curves on the dirt roads. I knew where she was going.

I pulled up next to her doing forty with the windows down, and tried to shout her into giving it up. She banged me off the road. When I got going again I was way back in her dust cloud. I choked through it, to the driveway for the Judge's ranch, and saw her taillight flaring as she braked by the house. Then I had to slow down and try to think. There

was a dry wash where my car wouldn't be seen. I hiked in
through the mesquites and across the trickling stream and
among the black shapes of the Judge's dozing cattle. I picked
up a stick in case of cattle or pit bulls and laughed at myself
and sneaked up to the house and flattened against the adobe
wall. Some pit bull was breaking pit-bull etiquette by bark-
ing out back by the dog yard. If anybody came out of the
house and wanted to they could blow me away. The old
Arizona howdy-do.

The dog shut up. The engine in Alice's pickup ticked
cool. She still hadn't gotten a hood for it. Things were
crawling in the ivy that had grown up the adobe. I sneaked
along to the corner of the front porch and dropped and
crawled out along it until I had an angle on the living-room
window. Alice was standing in there with her back to me.
Beside her was Larry the Rat. Over by the big stone fireplace
the Judge was facing both of them and me. He and Alice were
talking but the words didn't carry outside. Larry the Rat
went off to the kitchen and came back with a bottle of beer
and shoved it to Alice. The Judge talked and Alice swigged.
She stepped closer to him and answered. He made a fist and
socked his other hand, demanding. He demanded again.
Leisurely Larry the Rat took out a revolver and held it out
straight in both hands and pressed the barrel against Alice's
head. She ignored the gun and talked to the Judge, then
swung the beer bottle down slowly and tapped a pine-slab
table and swung the bottle up again and down hard and broke
it, splashing fragments and beer; now she was holding the
jagged neck of glass. Taking her own time she raised the
bottle neck and ground it into Larry the Rat's forearms and
hands, he didn't even fucking flinch, just took it, his blood
curling down the bottle and down her hand dripping onto the

floor. She got more serious working the broken glass and my nerves and finally he had to drop his left hand off the gun to grab her wrist, the two of them straining over the bottle neck, her two hands to his one, still keeping it sort of casual, no kicking or shifts in stance, Larry the Rat imploring the Judge — he wanted to pull the trigger on her. The Judge said something and Larry the Rat looked disgusted and swung the gun and his arms out of her reach. She held on to the bottle neck that was red now and said something final to the Judge and turned her back and walked to the door, speeding up as she opened it, bolting for her pickup with Larry the Rat coming fast behind her — if he looked my way I was had! — the flat gunshots and flames streaking from the barrel, whacking the night, shredding the front tires and dropping the cab. She was climbing out the far side with the shots still echoing off the hills and him sprinting after her. I stood up and yelled, "Sheriff's Department! Hold it right there!"

It stopped Larry the Rat and then I was running away too, through the mesquites and toward the road. I heard shots and saw the flashes and tore through those thorns and out to the road and then got taken down. A leg can scream! One of the pit bulls was on me, grinding in just below my knee, hotter than pain — tumbling me across the dirt — I rolled over and socked it, gouged at its leathery eyelids, crawled away dragging it — no good! — then Alice was there jabbing down with her broken bottle, the solid thumps as the glass penetrated the mass of it, the monster writhing, still clamped to me — get it off! My fingernails broke as I pried frantically to get leverage on the jaws, and when they finally gave with a socketing sound, Alice was still thumping down with the glass into the bloody unmoving mass. I got up and fell down and got up again with her helping me and we made it to the car. I gave her the keys and the back window exploded into fragments. More shots. She drove us out of range.

She raced us along the back roads, running off one side and then the other, over rocks and what passed for plants.

"Slow down! You're going to wreck us."

She floored it instead and fishtailed through a couple more curves and down a long straightaway past a sign telling us to slow for a hard right onto a one-lane bridge. She blasted the curve and went sideways going onto the bridge and smacked and rode the railing. Then we were across, skidding up on two wheels and almost over until we rocked to a stop off the road, and the engine died. I snatched the keys and got out and crumpled. Under my nose and running back under the bridge was a narrow canyon with rock walls that went down plenty far enough. My dogbite hurt like hell.

I started muttering curses and kept it up while she fetched stuff from the car, squatted down inside her draping hair and tugged my hands off the bite — a smile of bloody tooth-holes swelling and turning black — and sucked in her breath: "Beautiful." She cleaned it with water from a plastic jug, made a compress out of fast-food napkins, tore a rag out of my shirt and wrapped it on as a bandage, loosened the rag so the bite didn't throb as much. "We need some whiskey to pour over it."

I'd run out of obscenities but still I wasn't talking to her. I sat there, she stood, both of us staring down into the canyon. She said, matter-of-factly, "I told the Judge."

I fired a stone into the depths. "It's a long way down."

"That tape you and Rissler concocted, he knows it'll prove you set him up. He calls it evidence of a conspiracy. I held back telling him where it is. For now. Without the tape it'll just be his rantings and ravings . . . A court can find him

guilty or not. I know he's guilty and of what, and it won't
mean anything until I dish out his punishment personally
and make it permanent. I want you for my partner, Baby. You
call me that, I can too. Help me and I'll give you the tape and
deny the whole thing."

"You're a witch. A crazy whacko witch and I never
should've gotten this far with you."

"Don't tear us down, Macky — "

"Whacko! God, it feels good to come right out and say
it. You're a screwball! A flake! A freak! How many times
have you gone through this and with how many poor
chumps? Poor puppets! You got notches on your cunt? If you
want to so badly why don't you kill him all by yourself?
What do you need me for? You handled them pretty well
without me."

The hurt version of her now: "A half hour ago we were
saving each other's asses. You know we belong together." She
looked at me crookedly. "I can't be alone."

I beat her back with laughter that was as cruel as I could
make it. "Alice from the other side of the looking glass! Go
back where you came from!" She cringed at the edge of the
dropoff into the canyon.

Everything I hated and feared came down to her on the
edge of the dropoff. Madness? She had nothing on me!
"Jump!" I yelled. "Jump!"

She dropped her head and backed off the edge, tumbling
rocks under her knees and then her waist as she slid down,
her arms and hair trailing, slipping away from me.

I sprang for the edge and grabbed one of her hands and she
reached up with the other to beat on my grip, so I had to take
her full weight as she slipped down farther on the overhang
that wasn't quite vertical, her legs dangling over nothingness. Stones we dislodged started the long twisting plunge.

"Let me go, Macky!" Her voice echoed in the hollow of the little canyon.

"I should! I fucking should!"

She scraped against the rock and I heard her crying. Her face was hidden in the tangle of her hair. Her hand was slipping out of mine.

"Come back to me, Baby! I can't haul you up by myself."

She stopped struggling and hung from me, dead weight. "Just let go, Macky, and you'll be rid of me."

A pleading yell escaped from me: "Alice!"

In the dwindling echoes she got purchase with her knee and then the other one, and swung her other hand and grabbed mine. She did a scraping chin-up and I was glad — *glad!* — to see her fierce look back in place. Then I was staring past her at the bottom as she climbed up over me.

17

SHE HELPED ME back to the car and got us going at a more or less sane speed for once, and I lay down with my head in her lap. The desert rolled by, crooked plants and bare rock and dead sand, enchanted by moonlight. That's how a woman can make you see even Arizona. She stroked my forehead silently. But all the time she was working it out, and I knew she was and I couldn't do anything about it, hell, as wrong as it was I could manage a sort of perverse respect for her having the guts to want to pull it off. Most people lack that degree of dedication. Most people are dedicated to nothing anymore. If she was dedicated to murder, well, at least it was something. But I couldn't tell her that, I couldn't talk about it at all, or it might be real.

She just kept stroking me, one hand on the wheel as she drove and one hand fingering my neck, in my hair, rubbing my temple, tenderly pinching my earlobe, melting my shock and tension with her touch. I drifted and then lights were sweeping through the car at trippy angles. I sat up, disoriented, and saw we were coming into the city. Her lips parted as she stared ahead at the traffic, and as she turned to me my gaze focused on her teeth, like I was noticing them for the first time, suddenly fascinated at that aspect of her — and something let go in me. Her teeth stretched wider and larger and sharper. I turned away from them and there was a car coming at us on the left, a pair of headlights and a front grill yawning wide. I looked to the right at a spotlighted billboard where a local TV weatherman was gaping down at me with his gigantic grin . . . and at a cozy little house fenced by white-picket teeth . . .

Then we were at my place, her leaning over me inspecting my dogbite, the ugly punctures and wraparound bruise. That pit bull had given me a real Arizona kiss.

She soaked it in hot washcloths and swabbed on disinfectant and taped on a fresh bandage and lay me down and snuggled against me in bed. Like I've said, she had power. The next morning after I escaped to work she showed me more of it.

I got called into Burke's office. He had Rosie Garcia, the cop reporter, in there with him. They got right to it.

"There's some ugly information being circulated," Burke said. "Something about you and Rissler tipping off the Judge about the investigation, and inviting him to take a crack at you."

"Sure we did." That had them shifting around and staring at me. "Then we bought him a bucket and told him about the water gag. And we told him just where to have Rissler slapped so he'd go quickly."

"So there's nothing to it?"

"Of course not."

Rosie raised the black-frame rake-cornered glasses that were chained around her neck, slid them on, and jotted in her notebook. She was an old pencil nub under red-dyed hair that was cut short on her neck and sprayed to make sure she wouldn't have a curlicue anywhere on her, wrinkled and sunspotted in creased ditch-digger's pants and a white dress shirt with an iron-on patch showing inside a fraying shoulder seam, the chain-smoker's perpetual frown, the thick-lensed glasses exaggerating her seen-everything cop's eyes after thirty years on the beat for the combine. The joke about Rosie was she would've been a cop herself except she hated to get dressed up and thought donuts were too suggestive. It was fond legend that she lived alone except for a bilingual foul-mouthed parrot she fed vodka and trail mix to and a police scanner she kept squawking twenty-four hours a day so she could bolt to the scene of every new rape, murder and holdup. She'd solved more than a few; she was respected for that, and for the way she defined the human condition as blood and corruption and shit and maybe a bouquet dropped on the sidewalk here and there for journalistic relief. Some of the narrow-tie pups at the paper called her Officer Garcia behind her back, but to every cop in town and everybody else she was just Rosie. Nobody fucked with her.

I said, "What's she doing?"

"Rosie will be covering this," Burke said.

"Covering what?"

"The allegations and how we handle them."

"Stonewall them."

"We can't do that. The Judge put them on the record this morning. He's making it part of his defense."

Rosie puffed on her cigarette, blew a stream of smoke toward the door to the newsroom, said nothing.

"Come on."

"We have to issue a statement. This'll be news. He says you and Rissler called him up anonymously and encouraged him to come down to that barn and confront you."

I managed an ordinary laugh. I asked Rosie, "Did you take that down? Ha, ha, ha." I told Burke, "He can't have any evidence."

"He says he can get some. He says Alice Malone can verify the whole thing."

"I just tried to call her," Rosie said, hoarse as usual. "At your place? She didn't answer. Any idea where she is?"

"Check Burke's lunch calendar."

Burke reddened. "Cut the bullshit. She's living with you, that's bad enough. I warned you about your story not holding up."

"And this means it didn't? You can get some good practice, Burke. This is one reaction you get to a real story — when people are nailed, they'll try to squirm out of it any way they can. This is just the beginning. He'll call me a child molester if it might get him off."

"This sounds a little more believable."

"Give him that much credit."

Burke tried to read my face. "Okay. Work up a statement. This is getting around and we'll have to counter it."

"We should talk to Malone," Rosie said.

"I thought there was no smoking in here," I said.

"Set it up, Macky," Burke said.

"I will if I can. I don't set her schedule."

"Unless she skips town she'll have to talk about it."

"She wouldn't skip, would she?" Rosie said.

"Not unless she heard you were looking for her."

"Get that statement to Rosie right away," Burke said. "And then track her down. We need her on our side on this."

"I could just ask Macky some questions," Rosie said.

Burke looked at her. "You'd just be willing? Let's not make with the third-degree yet. Right now let's go with something prepared that we can be exact with and stick with. Do a draft and let me see it."

I got hold of a terminal and tapped out a one-sentence denial, and then the standard comeback, saying the Judge

must be desperate to fabricate such a wild charge. I made a
printout and showed Burke.

"Not very long, is it?"

"It shouldn't be. Any more than this would just give more
weight to what he's claiming."

Burke studied every word and of course had to diddle with
a few. He handed it back without looking at me. "Okay."

I delivered it to Rosie, who was taking notes on the phone.
"Does this change your view of the case?" she asked the
phone, and did some writing. "He's around somewhere. You
calling him in?" She did some more writing. "Her? . . . Yeah.
Yeah. You can't sit on it, can you? . . . Okay. If there's any-
thing to it, what would the charge be? Uh-huh . . . Hold on,
I'll take a look." She pushed the hold button and told me,
"Dunlap, down at the prosecutor's. He's asking for you.
Wants you to come in."

"Take a message."

Rosie stretched her lips sideways and nodded and got
back on with Dunlap. "He was here a while ago. I'll make
sure he gets told. Okay." She hung up. "He wants Malone
too. He's got a man over at your place watching for her. She
doesn't seem to be around."

"You having a good time?"

"It's what I get paid for."

I gave her the statement. She scanned it, said, "Aren't you
going to run through your side of it? He's got the time you and
Rissler supposedly made the call, what you supposedly
said."

"My side of it is the facts. Take them out of what's already
been printed."

The city desk secretary shouted, "Macky, oh-four."

"I'll take it over here." Of course it was the *Evening Error*,
wanting my comment. I read them the statement and said

that was it and they badgered me for more so I told them to
try Burke. Through the glass around his office I saw him pick
up the phone and talk for too long. The phones at city desk
went off.

"Macky, oh-two's for you."

"Macky, oh-five."

"Macky, they're all for you."

I took them one by one as they came in and gave them my
statement, and the ones that didn't like it I transferred to
Burke's line. They were from the TV stations and the Phoenix papers and then the wires and some bigger papers and
stations from out of state. I was on with some poor bastard
from radio when Rosie flopped the first edition of the *Evening
Error* down in front of me. It smelled of the presses and more.
THEY SUCKED ME INTO IT, JUDGE SAYS, front page. Underneath was what passed for the story. They had thirty inches of
the Judge going on with his charges, and how he never
intended to hurt anyone, and a recap from the files. They put
my denial up high to keep them out of a lawsuit but they
managed to make it look awfully lonely. On the jump page
they had Burke defending the paper and the original story
and saying he'd look into it anyway to make sure the highest
standards of journalism had been strictly adhered to, as the
Morning Mistake's readers could expect. The way it was put
together, half the readers wouldn't get that far, and the rest
would already be figuring me guilty. The *Evening Error* had it
right for once. The story had been aimed directly at me.

Very close to the blades of the combine now and if I went
down it would be an even better story; whoever got it first
would get the credit and maybe even a respite for a day or
two. There were plenty of them right on my own paper who

wouldn't mind seeing it happen, and some like Rosie who wanted to be in on it. I couldn't even blame them.

Even Burke. I wasn't going to level with him because it would just give him the excuse to play the man in charge. He'd be ordering the troops off in all directions, calling the lawyers about the possible angles and swearing he wouldn't give me up, and all the time he'd be figuring where his percentages lay; when it would make him look good, he'd give me up without a blink. He'd make it seem like he'd done all he could, furthered all sorts of principles of the profession, backed his man, and finally, reluctantly, taken the only responsible course. Then he'd be invited to speak at all the journalism conferences on the ethical dilemmas at stake. That would get his name out. That would put him at the top of the story. I wasn't going to give him the opportunity.

If what I'd done for the sake of journalism ever came out it would cost me my job, and what I called a career, and maybe more. Once the combine got done with me, I might end up riding a boxcar out of Arizona, if I could get out at all. Alice had even helped me write the headline: REPORTER NAILS HIMSELF.

I looked up into a TV crew shooting me right there in the newsroom. "How'd they get in here?" somebody asked. Their cutie-pie stand-up shoved her microphone and a question at me and I took the microphone and closed it in a drawer. A couple of our editors started hassling her and the crew and two security guards took sides. The videocam was getting it all down on tape. I went over to Burke and told him, "I'm getting out of here."

"They give this business a bad name. Better check in at

the prosecutor's. Dunlap wants you pretty bad. I'll have somebody from the firm go hold your hand."

"I don't need a lawyer."

"But I might."

I went down and out the back door. At the back gate of the lot there was another TV crew waiting to pounce. Floor it, Macky, get two or three of them, flick on the wipers and washers to clean off the spatter and that would be that. But not yet. Thread through them slowly, bye-bye, see you next time.

I stopped at a pay phone and tried Alice. No answer. After I hung up I could still hear the ringing ringing ringing tighter and tighter inside my head.

Stu Dunlap was one of these precisely bearded assistant prosecutors, the type who trim every hair one by one, and who want you to think they never did anything wrong, or even had an impure thought. He had the wire-rim glasses and a charcoal suit that looked like it had been unwrapped ten minutes ago, and a designer briefcase that didn't have a scuff on it. That was how you knew it was an act. Underneath all the goodness and propriety Dunlap was a real rabbit-puncher. He had to be. You can't go around nailing guys in court and sending them to the little gray rooms for twenty and thirty years at a crack without first getting rid of any impulses of humanity you might have. It would just slow you down. Sure, you can come up with a sympathetic glance at the victims of crime, if it'll tack on an extra decade or two to the sentence of the guy you are nailing. You can put a tremble in your voice and a glisten in your eyes while you're describing how the victims were just ruined if it might impress the jurors and make the evening news. You can do that much, but what you can't do is allow yourself to feel anything remotely like it. Otherwise you'd have trouble in court, where the first sign of any sort of weakness is as good as losing the whole case. And trouble in court means career trouble, the one thing no prosecutor can risk. Not with half of them on their way to Washington or at least the state capital, willing to do anything to get there, willing to nail anyone, to declare war on drugs and war on permissiveness and war on everyone who ever stepped out of line, and of course, when it fit the script, war on journalism.

Which is where I came in. Dunlap and I had been through a few go-rounds, with him trying to force me to turn over notes and negatives and reveal confidential sources, and me, back when I was working with words, trying to show him up for distorting evidence to suit his cases — coaching witnesses, goading the lab techs into overreaching on a fingerprint match or a rape exam, that sort of thing. The usual stuff, none of it ethical, the public at large not really giving a damn as long as everyone accused got nailed and sent away.

This time I was the accused. Not formally, maybe, but Dunlap played it that way. He'd been one of them pressing for copies of the dogfight photos and he was pressing the case against the Judge and now he was back pressing me. He had me hauled into an interrogation room, a bare place except for a little picture of the Grand Canyon thumbtacked in the center of one wall. He stood over me and made me tell all over again my version of the night Rissler got killed.

"What were you doing about eight o'clock?"

"Getting ready to shoot the dog ring at the barn."

"Who was with you?"

"Rissler came over sometime around then. Alice Malone was in and out."

"You sleeping with her?"

"Is that what you call it? That doesn't bear on this."

"It does if she was one of your sources on this dogfight investigation."

"You know anything like that is confidential."

"Excuse me! Go down with a source and hide behind the journalist's code. It won't be confidential if she'll talk."

"So ask her."

"Did you make any calls around this time?"

"What time?"

"Eight o'clock."

"I don't know. I guess I could have, or maybe Rissler did, or Alice. I was busy packing my cameras."

"Why did Rissler have to be along?"

"You knew him. You have to ask?"

"You say you wanted to rig these remote cameras to be in position for the next dogfight? Seems pretty complicated."

"Maybe, to somebody not in the business."

"Most people in the business don't operate like you do, Macky."

"Thanks."

"Why'd the Judge stop in?"

"Ask him. Get to the point, Dunlap. I've heard the allegations."

"They make a lot more sense than the way you tell it."

"They do if all you're interested in is nailing me."

"I'm interested in all sorts of things. I'm obtaining a subpoena for your phone records. They'll show toll calls for that night — it's long-distance out to the Judge's ranch, isn't it? The phone records will give me more than allegations."

That managed to rouse the paper's lawyer — Cass Unger again, who wasn't happy about being there to represent me. She told Dunlap getting that subpoena might not be so easy, and they went around on that and didn't settle anything

except what high-level ass-kickers they were. Then Dunlap
started in on me again.

"You want to tell me about that call?"

"What call?"

"You and Rissler to the Judge."

"If Rissler called him, I didn't hear it."

"You'll put it off on him."

"There's nothing I have to put off on anyone."

"I've been phoning your place all day. Don't you have an
answering machine?"

"I did when I left this morning."

"Isn't it working?"

"I don't know. I haven't tried it lately. I didn't mind being
out of touch with all this publicity."

"You mind if we go over there now and take a look at it?"

"Why? You handling the warranty? Is this the best excuse
you can come up with to get in the door? Maybe I mind you
sniffing my old shoes."

"I might. If you had the tape stashed in one of them."

"What tape?"

"The one from your answering machine, that you and
Rissler played for the Judge."

"You on drugs, Dunlap?"

"I'll get a warrant and see for myself. Hey, that's pretty
good. Warranty, warrant. This isn't going to hold together for
you. It's going to come apart. I'm going to take it apart."

"Let him strut," I told Unger. She sat back.

"I argued my first case before Harker," Dunlap said.

"That's why they call him the Judge."

"He stood for something."

"From a distance, maybe."

"He got old and when that happens it isn't only your ears

and your nose that grow too big. On the Judge it's his opinion of himself and what he can get away with. He fucked up royally and I'm not looking the other way or cutting any deal to reduce the charges against him. I'm charging him up the ass. But if his account of things sounds better than yours I'm charging you up the ass too. It's my responsibility to the public."

"Go ahead."

"If you were scheming and contributed in any manner to Rissler's death, that's accessory to murder."

"Doesn't sound as bad as turning over a source, or cooperating with a prosecutor." I got up, pointed at the little thumbtacked picture. "What's that doing in here?"

"This is the Grand Canyon State. You don't like the scenery?"

"Is that all?"

"Your leg giving you trouble? What's wrong with it?"

"I got beat up, remember?"

"It bothers you this long after? Couldn't it be more recent? Like a dogbite from last night?"

"No."

He bent over and pinched my pantleg. "That painful? Got it bandaged, that size, it could be a dogbite. Like from a pit bull maybe? The Judge had one of his killed last night. He thinks it tore into somebody first. Just one detail of his account."

Unger said, "Let go of his leg."

Dunlap straightened up. "I'll get a warrant for that too. For Macky to drop his pants. Unless you'd like to volunteer."

"Let's draw out the excitement," I said.

"You'll have to hang around."

"This is bush-league harassment," Unger said. "Nobody's going to grant you anything on this lard."

Dunlap took his briefcase and Unger followed him out. I looked at the bare walls and the little Grand Canyon. There was a fly buzzing and I snatched it on the second try and then let it go. I snatched it three times before Unger came back.

"Let's go," she said. "Dunlap's full of lard." But the way she looked at me said different.

Out in the hallway, of course, we ran into Alice. She clutched my arm and did the routine.

"Macky, are you all right? Did they torment you? I was so worried." She forced a kiss on me. "Is there anything I can do?"

There was a prosecutor's man with her. "We'll tell you what to do," he said.

"He was at the house," Alice said. "He said I didn't have to come but when I heard they had you in here I couldn't stay away. What should I tell them?" She looked at the prosecutor's man and let me go and let him take her over. "I'll tell them just how it happened. Everything. They won't have a thing against you then."

The prosecutor's man took her down the hallway and they linked up with Dunlap. The three of them disappeared into the interrogation room.

"I could go in there," Unger said. "She'd have to ask."

"She doesn't need any help."

"If they start in with the torment?"

"She enjoys torment."

"She dresses for it . . . If they rape her in there, I'll take the case defending them."

"I thought you women were sticking together these days."

"Where'd you hear that?" She thumbed at the door where

Alice had disappeared, then tapped the bandage on my leg, making me flinch. "We need to talk."

"Why? So you can report back to Burke?"

"You'll regret treating me this way." But she left.

I sat on a bench by the elevators and waited for Alice. It wasn't much of a wait . . .

Dunlap came out of the interrogation room followed by Alice and the other man. Dunlap looked down the hallway at me and then walked the other way. Alice patted the prosecutor's man and said something that made him laugh and came toward me.

"Let's go, Baby," she said. "Unless you'd like to move in."

We rode down in the elevator and the prosecutor's man rode with us. Alice leaned into me and said in a loud whisper, "I didn't tell them." The prosecutor's man stared at us.

18

LIKE AN UNDERCURRENT, my objections began to shift from *why* we weren't going to kill him, to *how* we weren't. Maybe what did it was being closed inside that interrogation room, with nothing to look at but that little Grand Canyon, and seeing the future if Alice turned me in. Or maybe it was just her. In Arizona you can live with a woman who wants you to commit murder, and be worried about losing her. You can start to think, subconsciously at first and then maybe more deliberately, of murder as not all that bad, compared to the alternatives. You can work it out logically like I tried to.

If I didn't do it, she would turn me in. If I threw her out, she'd turn me in. Both of which meant the end of me, my job, my reputation, and maybe my simulated freedom. So if I was going to murder anyone, maybe I should just murder her. But not her. *Not her.* I lived inside her, breathing her, drinking her. She was my mystery that I didn't want to solve or ever do without. That routine, only now I'd lost my detachment and was trapped in it, and I'd have to find out just how thoroughly I didn't give a damn.

I went out to my rock to do a jump, to get some distance and think things through. For once I walked to the edge of

the drop-off and looked down. It didn't scare me at first —
then it did. I got a little dizzy, too aware of every little move I
made. I walked back to the car and lined myself up. This
jump seemed like something I'd never done before. I got
myself running, as best I could limping on my dogbite, the
hell with it, and dived over the edge; the yell lasted forever
until the main chute caught me. I wasn't smart enough to not
pop it. That would've solved everything. I hit and rolled and
got up tingling, still focused on every move, deep in my guts,
falling, falling.

Hiking back to the car took no effort at all. I felt like
somebody else, a stranger — it wouldn't leave me alone.

Why the hell not play with the thought? If anyone deserved killing, the Judge did. He'd more or less killed Rissler, hadn't he? Wasn't he standing between me and a
Pulitzer? Hell, he was crusty enough that he might even see
something in the idea himself. He might choose to go out
that way, if he had to go, and everybody does. Wasn't I
feeling low enough to do it? — blaming myself for Rissler,
for getting mixed up with her, and figuring I might as well
prove just how low I could be. Get down, Macky.

"Well, Baby?"
"Well what?"
Nothing was ever more dangerous than her little smile.
We were lying together at my place that afternoon ignoring
the phone. Up in the foothills at an overlook for sunset.
Walking in the park that night under a dragging moon.
"I love you, Baby. Do this with me."
Twisted in the damp sheets on the bed next to her in the
long seconds around midnight. One sound emerging: her
breathing, sawing at me. The freeze-frames: lingering long
shot, her facedown in the sheets, her contours taunting,

hide-and-seek from toes to buttock to fingertips against the wrinkles of pale white cotton; close-up, her shoulder blade and upper arm at a right angle, and in the cavern underneath, the soft bulge of her breast mashed against the flat fitted sheet; close-up, isolating the secret underside of her foot, the plump toe pads and sole creased with ancient writing, and then another, framing her upper thigh where it met her flank — the invitation!; and as she stirred and shifted a leg and resettled, the capper: a medium shot of abandon, her darkness of tangled hair and arms outflung — all dominated by the bars of light that fell through the blinds.

Feeling my eyes on her, she roused and started in on me again.

"I'll do it by myself then, Macky. You told me to. I'll do it and if I get caught it'll all blow up."

She wanted to shoot him. She wanted to go get a gun, then do it. That's the kind of instant gratification we go for in Arizona. There's a gun store on every other corner, all stocked to start a few nice little wars — just walk in light and walk out heavy, they might as well be giving derringers away in cereal boxes to get all the kiddies started early. I told her she was thinking like a punk.

"What, walk up to him and start blasting?"

"I'll ambush him at his ranch. He takes hikes out there every morning."

"And when he turns up perforated by all these bullets, who'll they come for? Who's got a motive?"

"Anybody," she said. "Some dogfighter who got busted and thinks the Judge burned him. Some friend of Rissler's who wants payback. Or one of your paper's loyal readers getting fanatical over the editor's death and the decline it's caused on the comics page. Some loony friend of Big Ed's.

There'd be more suspects than me or you. Look at all the punks out shooting up the desert."

"We'd still be at the top of the list."

"I don't care if I'm caught. As long as I get him."

"Baby, you'd care. You'd be locked away with losers and without a man for a long, long time, if they didn't give you the gas. They still use cyanide — it's the Arizona perfume."

"I wouldn't care about anything but not having you, Macky." I could scoff at that and still want to believe it! "Then think up a better way," she said. "You're a journalist. You know all about murder."

"This isn't some goddamn story now, Alice."

That's how you approach an idea like this — you sneak up on it and touch it and back away, sneak up from another angle and touch it for a little longer, then back away again. Enough of that and maybe you can hold it long enough to give it a good look. Even then you don't know if you'll go through with it. It's an exercise in scaring yourself.

I got more tingly talking around it with her, trying to stall her by making it a puzzle to solve, and raising the hairs on my neck with a peek at what the solution would mean. I kept coming back to the Judge and his hikes.

"Is he pretty regular about them?"

"Every day, right at dawn."

"Where does he go?"

"Back behind his place, into the hills. Five miles."

"How can you say so exactly?"

"He's got a path and he clocks himself. Sometimes he goes farther, but never less than that. He says it takes that long to get his blood going."

"He does this alone?"

"He took me along a couple of times. I've still got cactus

in places I can't reach." She snorted. "He always takes
Devil. Since I stopped going with him, it's just him and the
dog. He likes to listen to the birds."

"It's all open land?"

"National forest, I think."

Which in Arizona, of course, usually means no forest at
all, just cactus and sand and maybe sparse mesquites. "Regular desert?"

"Very."

"Ever run into any snakes out there?"

"I never did. He talked about seeing them."

"Rattlers?"

Her giggle.

For rattlesnakes in Arizona go to a rattlesnake salesman,
but it's a little tricky, they don't operate in the open —
poisonous snakes are one of those natural Arizona treasures
protected by law. Which of course only ups the price and
demand, for rattlers as pets and rattlers as status symbols.
Everybody wants to throw a rattler party. It all guarantees the
black market. Every now and then a rattlesnake salesman
does get busted, but they're never out of business long —
the penalties are small and the rewards too great. I'd fed the
combine a few rattler-market stories about how terrible the
situation was, so I knew where we could put ourselves
through the next little test by trying to get some rattlers to go.

Around two A.M. we drove in Alice's pickup to a run-down
homestead northwest of town, where even the desert looked
run-down. There was an old stucco house, its broken corners
and cracks doubly severe under the glaring yardlight, and out
back among the shadows and tumbleweeds, some gap-
slatted sheds and an old cowboy trailer with its windows

sealed off by plywood. Prime habitat for a rattlesnake salesman. This one was named Cheney. He'd been busted a
while back and I'd been out shooting for the paper. I didn't
want to meet him again, because he might recognize me, and
I was just beginning to admit there was a very slight
chance . . .

I had Alice park a quarter mile down the county dirt road,
and let the air out of one of the tires. Then we walked to
Cheney's driveway. I hid in the desert and Alice went on to
the house. She pounded on the door and Cheney came out,
looking run-down too. He'd gone just about all the way bald,
compensating with a scraggly beard, and had his shirt off to
show his gut. Alice played him, and pretty soon Cheney went
inside and came out with a shirt on and a can of beer for her
and one for himself. They got into Cheney's pickup, which
was about as bad as Alice's except it had a hood, and drove
out the driveway, and started down the road. She would get
Cheney to change her tire and she'd keep him down there for
a guaranteed half hour. I'd have to be done by then, one way
or the other.

I circled around the reach of the yardlight and back to the
cowboy trailer. The door was padlocked. There was a length
of angle-iron in a scrap pile that worked just fine on the hasp.
Inside the trailer was cramped and dark and smelly. I swallowed a rise of panic and used a flashlight on the snakes. He
had them in glass cases on shelves, crowding me, each case
holding five or six or a dozen rattlers, lethargic and coiled
around each other. Some of them stuck up their heads and
stared at my light and flicked their tongues. I had two burlap
sacks and welders gloves and a pair of long barbecue tongs.
Get on with it, Macky. I began to sort through the snakes and
pick up ones that looked good and full of venom and sacked

them. They rattled and it caught on until all of them were rattling in all the cases; the sound got sharper and just about drove me out. I had to stop, close my eyes tight and clench myself and then ease off and start again. I squeezed maybe a little too hard with the tongs so as not to drop any, loaded a dozen in one sack and tied it off, then loaded the other sack, tucked away the gloves and tongs and flashlight, and got out of there with a sack of rattlers in each hand. Always balance your load in rattlers — a nugget of Arizona wisdom.

As I hiked out my sacks rattled and so did the whole trailer behind me, but the rattling got less loud, and then it was just one or two of them in the sacks. Finally they quit. I hid by the road until Cheney pulled in and then Alice drove by slowly in her truck. I stepped out and dropped the sacks in the bed and got in next to her.

"You get bit?"

"No. How about you?"

"Fatso tried. I could've used those tongs."

We drove around with the load of rattlers, not talking, just realizing that we'd come this far and there was only one more step to take. Were we going to take it, were we going to make the big jump over the last edge, or not? She had to work herself into it too, even after all her pushing and giggling and threats. She pulled over and let the engine idle and folded her arms over the steering wheel and her head down on her arms. She was breathing from her waist up. She rubbed those old cigarillo burns on her belly.

"One time," she said, "he locked me in the meat locker and didn't come back for hours and then wanted to make it while I was cold. Another time he tried to hang me. He was very selective. He could do things with the silverware or a toothbrush or a plastic comb." She looked at me. "He made me like it."

There was no wind but I felt it rushing in my ears. She started driving again, anywhere. "That's why."

So, fuck it. Murder isn't that hard. Not really. Most people who try get away with it. The hardest part is working yourself into it, but if you think about it long enough you can do it, just to stop the thinking, and you'll have reasons, good ones, because there are plenty against anybody. You can get steely and almost forget how it makes you feel deep inside. You can begin to see murder as just another job.

I'll tell it to you from the Judge's point of view.

Another beautiful Arizona morning. He's out there hiking. The sun just off the mountains, and already hot enough to have him sweating through the khaki shirt and shorts. Four miles out from the ranch house, hitting his stride, with the pit bull Devil ranging ahead. The path packed-down, dusty, showing no trace of rain — the desert has sucked it all up and now things are as they had been before, as they usually were. Up another little hill and down to a level outcropping of rock and there right in the path is something shiny, a canister, a cookie jar? Devil sniffs it. Somebody dropped it or left it there most likely, the way it's sitting upright in the middle of the path. A good-size chrome can with the lid on and stamped in red letters on the side, COOKIES. Like a scene out of Lewis Carroll. Devil acting funny. What the hell is it? Pick up the can, heavy, shake it, try to get the lid off. *Oh* —

One rattler kissed him on the cheek. It hung there from its fangs and he spun around shouting and swatting until it dropped off. He sat down and felt where his cheek was bleeding.

"Goddamn."

He found his hat lying next to him and put it on. Devil whipped into the snakes, there had been two coiled in the can, flung them down and chewed their heads off. The Judge stood up and staggered a few steps.

"Goddamn."

Devil came over to him, limping on a front leg where he'd been bitten. "You too, eh, boy? Go on, go home. Make it home, Devil." Hearing the strained voice, Devil didn't want to leave, he just limped halfway up the hill toward the ranch, and then limped back. "Go on, go on. Go home." Slowly, looking back often, Devil limped up the hill and over. The Judge used his canteen to douse his face, gingerly rinsed the fang marks.

"Goddamn."

He kicked the COOKIES jar. He stared hatefully around at the desert, and started up the hill, measuring each step.

"Don't want to rush a snakebite. Goddamn."

Alice and I got up from where we were hiding and joined him.

19

COOKIES," the Judge said. He shook his head and stumbled past us and labored up the hill. We fell in beside him. "You stashed yourselves upwind, I take it. You must have dunked that shiny can in something so Devil wouldn't smell the snake. Must have cut off the rattles. Didn't hear a thing. Thought it might be money in there. Or maybe cocaine. You thought of that."

Without breaking stride he pointed at what I had: a baseball bat. "Devil comes back, that won't do you much good."

Nothing could touch me. "We'll see."

"The way he's snakebit, it might be a contest. Most of the poison usually goes out in the first bite. He might not be slowed down much at all. You could use that bat on me."

"You'd like that, wouldn't you?" Alice said.

"I'll talk to you," the Judge told me. "And you better listen. No use dealing with her. She lives somewhere we can't get to."

Alice made a little noise and shoved him down. He was that weak already, or in shock. He was sweating more than the heat warranted and the skin was tugging back from his face. "I'll make it back," he said. His hat fell off again, and he squinted up at us. "It'll take more than a rattler to do me in."

He got up slowly and left his hat behind and moved stiffly up the hill. "Can't bruise me up or leave any marks."

"Falling down is all right," I told him. "You'd be doing that."

"She told you tales, didn't she? You fool."

"Let's run," Alice said. She took his arm and turned him around and ran him back down the hill. I picked up his hat and trailed them. He was bent over, panting.

"I was at Guadalcanal," he said. "*That* was difficult."

"Come here," she said. "You better rest." Draping his arm over her shoulder she walked him off the path, to the place we'd picked out: a hollow below a couple of big boulders. There was an overhang and a bed of loose rocks where snakes might den. She eased him down on the rocks. His cheek had blackened around the bite and that side of his neck was purple.

"I'm all right now," he rasped. "You can go. I'll see you later."

I tossed his hat down next to him. She took out one of the burlap sacks from where we'd stashed them and untied the sack and he yelled and tried to scramble away, and she dumped the rattlers on his legs and jumped back. He changed his yell to a whistling and kicked savagely; three or four struck him, and he beat them off with a rock. The others coiled up around him, rattling. Another one struck him and he smashed it. He was still whistling. He stared at the snakes and they rattled and fixed their snakes' eyes on him.

"Alice Delgado," he said. He whistled some more and tried to ease away from the snakes. When another one struck him, he tried to smash it and missed. He lay back on his elbows and ignored the snakes and rasped some more stuff at us: "They'd be in here, under the rocks and in the shade. They like to doze in big colonies. They can live with each other closely like that." Then again, more weakly: "Alice Delgado."

Shut your eyes, old man!

He did, as she dumped the second bag of snakes on his chest. One or two more struck him — the rest slithered off, and coiled and rattled. He looked at us and kept up the whistling.

"You did a good job investigating me," he said. "*Me.*" He reached for his hat, and got bit on the hand. He kept reaching and got the hat and put it on. He lay flat with his head on a rock and the hat shading his eyes. His legs twitched. "Breaking the law and no quality control. Sorry about your pal Rissler. That was accidental. Sorry about Ed too. He was with me sixteen years."

"You're a sorry son of a bitch," I said.

He twitched all over and doubled up on his side and got bit some more and hugged himself. "Burns," he said.

He laughed his laugh, like he knew a real Arizona joke.

"Macky!" The pit bull Devil ran down the hill for us. He was a fraction too slow and woozy and I got him on the first swing with the bat and beat him down until he was still.

The sun got a lot hotter. In a frenzy we brushed out our tracks where the ground wasn't rock and packed everything up and left the Judge there with the rattlers. He didn't seem to be breathing. Hampered by my old dogbite, I had to carry out Devil's body — and it was heavy.

We cut cross-country to Alice's pickup and stowed the dead pit bull in the back and drove thirty miles on dirt roads over the county line. We dumped the dog and then ran over it.

"Hit it again," I told her. She did. We left it there in the weeds beside the road. It would be just another dog found like that, or consumed by coyotes and buzzards. Farther on we flung out the burlap sacks and the baseball bat and then we drove back around the Santa Catalinas and up the pass between the range and the next range south.

"This is it."

We stopped and parked among some other cars and trucks and had more of what passed for conversation.

"Do you have the blanket?"

"It's in the red bag."

We went through the motions, the script we'd worked out, carrying our props down into a canyon that was a real Arizona paradise because during the summer rainy season the stream actually had water in it. It was popular with kids who chugged beer and turned up their boom-boxes too loud, and then died tumbling off the slickrock into the shallow pools or getting sucked over the series of cascades. Down at the paper, we'd had to go out on so many stories and shoot so many bodies getting dredged up and hauled out of there by ropes or helicopter that we'd taken to calling the place Search and Rescue Canyon.

Alice and I picked out a pool where the boom-boxes were at a low boom and stripped down to swimsuits and waded in. The plan was to have an alibi, just in case, but not one so good that it looked suspicious. I'd taken another day off, that's all. Yeah, that's all. Anyway, it was too late to do it any differently. The water was just wet, and wading in it made me more nervous — you can get like that about water after years in the desert — and I got out pretty quick. Finally Alice got out, and lay down next to me on a blanket. She still wasn't talking about it, and I wasn't asking.

Maybe you think we should have been savoring our black success. But it wasn't like that. There was too much not to remember, and not to think about, especially that one thing that had come up unexpectedly, and there's always one of those, isn't there? We were quiet, and extra polite with each other when we had to talk, and underneath everything, tense. I wondered if, from then on, we would ever not be.

We put in our time at Search and Rescue Canyon and then moved our not-guilty act out to the county fairgrounds. They have a fair every couple of months to cash in on the cotton-candy crowd. This one was typical. The highlight was the chicken-drop, where everybody surrounds a couple of chickens on a checkerboard, and you bet on which chicken will shit first and on exactly which square the shit will fall on. It's the quintessential Arizona entertainment, the chicken-drop.

I lost twelve bucks and then we gave up and went back into town. There was no story in the *Evening Error*, which had gone to press before noon, but the wires had put out a bulletin. We hadn't been home for ten minutes before the more obsessed journalists were calling me for comment, which, trying to sound reserved, I declined to give. Then Burke called.

"You heard about the Judge? We're doing a weeper. You and Rosie better handle it. Your name belongs on the story. The readers will look for it, and it'll demonstrate how the paper is squarely behind you on this. Get out there to his ranch and get with the deputies. I want pictures of where it happened, what they're doing — the body if you can get it."

Burke hung up. Without meeting her eyes any more than I had to I told Alice. She said flatly, "You can't."

"They don't give comp time for murder. I have to act normal and do this."

"You're just trying to get away from me. Go ahead. It wasn't my idea to use rattlesnakes or to run over the dog twice."

Then we had to hold each other, but not for long. I drove out there and pretty soon I was looking down at the spot where we'd done it. Scattered around were a lot of dead rattlers that the deputies had mashed. They had the Judge's body off to the side, in the shade of one of the boulders, and were just sealing it inside a body bag and belting it to a stretcher. I shot the body and the dead snakes and then some deputy killing another snake with a stick while others watched.

"That's not a rattler, Sammy. It's a gopher snake. It won't hurt you."

"I don't care. I hate them."

Some of the deputies were scouting around for other evidence, and I shot them too. One or two who'd been tight with the Judge, or with his law-and-order image, didn't like me doing it, and turned their backs.

"Aren't you satisfied yet, Macky? You blow the guy up all over the paper and maybe he misses his step because of it and now you've got to come out here and blow him up again."

"Take it easy, Al."

"He's worse than these snakes."

They kept each other off me. Enough of them appreciated my work and didn't mind a little nailing as long as it was done accurately. But they kept their distance and so did I, because a journalist who has friends isn't doing the job. I shot them all. I got a good shot of one of them looking desert-beaten, his hat off, wiping his face under the sun. And I got the standard shot of Larry the Rat weeping. He'd found the body. One more surprise — those tears. He saw me shooting him, and the deputies had to hold him back. "It's easy for you now, isn't it?" he said. "It's so fucking easy."

Then Rosie Garcia found me, and I shot her bumming a smoke from a deputy and lighting it up, her eyes concealed behind the prescription sunglasses chained around her neck, as clunky as her regular pair. "A real pro, aren't you, Macky?"

"We can use you on the fashion page. The dinosaur look."

"I knew you'd want to be here. That's why I asked Burke to send you. Hell of a deal, isn't it? What a way to go."

"I've got what I need," I told her. "Let's split."

"Let's let them finish looking. You can never tell."

So we sweated it out, which gave Rosie the chance to needle me some more: "I'd think you'd be doing handsprings. Now that the Judge is out of it, you're in the clear."

"I was in the clear before."

"I mean, now there's nobody to take up his side of it. Unless you count Dunlap."

"I like working with you, Rosie."

"You don't subscribe to the creative-tension theory?"

Finally one of the deputies came over and said, "We're calling it off. Only went this long because we can't locate the dog. He must've gotten bit too, or maybe he ran off. Can't figure out where he's got to."

"That is strange," Rosie said.

"He'll turn up," the deputy said.

"Yeah," I said.

That's all it took to trigger the gruesome freeze-frame memories: Devil in mid-leap bent around the blur of the bat, his eye-whites showing and his jaws flailing open and teeth flopping; the first rattler dangling from the Judge's cheek, a surreal streamer as he danced; close-up of the writhing mass of snakes dropping on his chest as he pursed his lips to whistle; the telescopic shot I'd just taken of the body, the bloated thing of taut black skin dappled with puncture wounds; and back into forbidden memory for the close-up of

Alice's face, her expression — yeah! — bracketed by her raised arms as she dumped the rattlers on her victim. Our victim!

Rosie had my arm, steadying me, peering into my face.

"A little dehydrated," I said.

"You almost fainted."

I shrugged her off.

We made a two-car caravan back to the newsroom. It was fully mobilized and when you see a newsroom like that you can actually think something is getting accomplished. Burke had a team doing the background on the Judge's career and the dogfighting and another team calling half the people in town for sentimental comments.

I should've figured. A weeper gets done on anybody important who dies and some not important at all except in how they died or why they died, like saving a baby in a fire or shooting down bankers come to repossess the farm. The standard form requires quotes from the deceased's neighbors and pals and maybe family, about what a great and sensitive guy he was, how he played with kids in the park every weekend and adopted stray cats and never uttered an unkind word about anyone. That sort of helium. If you called around and found out the guy stomped cats and spit on his neighbors, okay, you still did a weeper, but taking the angle that here had been a man not at peace with himself. So sad. That was the basic tone in words and pictures. Once you had the act of a casket salesman down, you could work the survivors and sell it all to the readers. Of course — get it, Macky? — not many journalists had done weepers on guys they'd killed.

I had to hustle out some prints of the death scene and then help Rosie. She was taking all the notes from the other reporters, moving them in blocks on the computer, tapping out the story, weaving everything together. I pulled up a chair next to her and now and then offered advice that she didn't want.

"We could move up his description. Look at this file shot."

"He was western," Rosie said. She tapped it in.

"And look at these deputies. This give you any inspiration?"

Rosie tapped in that the deputies had pushed themselves to exhaustion, then she saw how that knocked everything down a whole extra line, and she fiddled with the wording, until the deputies were just tired, and Rosie had saved a tenth of an inch. Around us some of the others were still calling for comments.

"I'm sorry to have to do this, ma'am. That's right, from the *News-Gazette*. No, we aren't persecuting him. We just report the news. Well, before you hang up, can you offer us a few words on how he'll be missed? I see . . . 'A good man. Better than any airhead journalist.' Yes, I've got it."

"Hello, yes, this is the *News-Gazette*. Yes, that's why. What was it like being his bailiff for nine years? No, we're not digging dirt. Just anything you want to tell us. He used to do what? Did he use a toothpick or just his fingernails?"

"And how was his health, doctor? Yes, I know you can't say exactly. How about generally? Had he been depressed? Yes, I know everybody is, but was he maybe a little more depressed than average?"

They took it all down and moved it to Rosie and she inserted it where she had room. A couple of them were working with the art department on tables listing key dates and facts from the Judge's rise and downfall, and the M.E. for graphics was cursing on the phone to the press room demanding color. Suzy Kino delivered a handful of mugshots she'd taken of the sources and said, "The duly bereaved."

All day I'd been screaming at myself to hold on — just get through it, don't puke, don't scream out loud, they don't suspect, and don't think about the other thing! Finally I got up dizzy and told them I was taking a break. Rosie didn't look up from her screen, only asked, "What does a nest of rattlers look like?"

"What?"

"I need an adjective. Thought you might have one."

"Seething."

She tapped it in. "Take your time," she said.

There was no chance of that. I'd been thinking around it but I couldn't do that anymore. I had to know.

I got past everyone and ducked into the library. A clerk asked me if I needed help and I said no. I checked the clips and then went back to the microfiches. There she was: Alice Delgado. I put her up on one of the viewers. Fourteen years ago she'd been a very big story. As big as this time around, maybe bigger.

20

HER TRIAL had lasted three weeks, front page every day. There had been enough shots of what they could get back then, her climbing in and out of cars escorted by deputies or matrons of the court. A little girl, ten years old, but if you looked close, the same long black hair and fierce looks. Testimony had covered what her father had done to her, and the effect it would've had on a girl her age, and how she couldn't be blamed. He had raised her up hard and used her and done things to her that couldn't be printed in a family newspaper, even for Arizona families. One day she waited for him to come home and there had been testimony about how the neighbors heard the shotgun go off and how she came outside and walked down the center of the street dragging it. He'd been an investigator for the tax department and of course he'd always kept his desk neat and the dirt in his yard raked. She'd confessed to killing him and also to killing her mother, which turned for the defense, because her mother had in fact died giving birth to her. Shrinks had been brought in to contradict each other about how her mind worked and didn't work and exactly what she was thinking when she squeezed the trigger, jacked in a new round and squeezed again, and whether she really deserved to be con-

victed of first-degree murder. The presiding judge who'd
had to sort it all out, double of course, had been Leo Aloysius
Harker.

There was even an editorial after the verdict, offering a
little praise for mercy — the Judge had ruled her not guilty
by reason of insanity, and ordered her into the state mental
hospital until such time as she showed signs of recovery and
the ability to lead a normal life. There was no follow-up about
how she had eventually gotten out anyway.

The editorial blurred in front of me and the fan inside the
microfiche viewer got louder and louder — the wind from the
long jump. Freefall. Or what about the approaching roar of
the journalism combine? Which is it, Macky? You've been
mixing metaphors and committing other crimes.

I got up and tipped over my chair and then righted it with
some of them looking at me. I made myself walk, to finish
out this little scene. The clips on the Judge were heaped in
the tray up front, ready to be refiled after all the reporters had
gone through them. They hadn't been converted to microfiche yet — five or ten clips could be reduced onto a single
fiche, so the library was changing over to save space, but
slowly, starting with the oldest files, not following any particularly logical system, doing a little here and there when the
combine let up for a moment. I found the envelope for the
year of the trial and shuffled through it. FOR BACKGROUND ON
ALICE DELGADO CASE, SEE MICROFICHE, REFERENCE HER. A
plain white index card. There was another card referencing
another case transferred to microfiche. I'd gone right by the
cards that first day she'd sicced me on the Judge — in a hurry
as usual. I'd been in a hurry for years. Newspaperman. I
crumpled one of the cards, uncrumpled it and shoved it in the
face of the nearest clerk. "What is this?"

I yelled, "What is this?"

"We're down two positions with the budget cut like it is and microfiching takes time and money. Files like this, we sift out the stuff that doesn't seem that important and put it on fiche, and leave the rest in clips where it's easier to get at." She pointed her chin and got sarcastic. "It's part of our ongoing effort to modernize."

"Macky, what're you hollering about?" Burke. I got back to the microfiche viewer and switched it off before he could get a good look. "What's this? You raiding the archives?"

"Just checking something."

"Hustle it up. We've got the page proofs and you better look them over."

"I'll clean up here and be right out."

"I want those presses rolling." He shot me a look and left. I straightened the clips and the stack of microfiches and pocketed the fiche on Alice. One of the clerks was watching me.

I went out and looked at the proof they had worked up for the next morning's front page. RATTLERS KILL DOGFIGHTING EX-JUDGE. It didn't exactly sing, but it had the facts. The simulated facts. There was no mention of murder or any evidence that pointed to anyone or anything but that seething nest of rattlers.

Disappointed, Macky? You pull it off and then get written out of the story! Even a killer likes a little credit for what he's done! *Absurd?!* Yeah, I could think like that. I could have a sense of humor about it because what the hell else did I have, now? And hadn't the Judge gone down laughing? I could tell myself all sorts of good Arizona jokes, about Alice and her men, and how I could put together a much, much better story than what was in front of me, if I was only willing to take a little thing like a murder rap. Maybe it'd be worth it for the best shot at a Pulitzer.

Burke had me read all the proofs, the weeper, the side-bars, the photo cutlines, everything. It was just what the combine liked to spit out, no rough corners, a good package. In the morning a hundred and fifty thousand stiffs would glance at it over coffee and think they had been touched.

Too fast, then too slow, drawing horn honks, blowing at least one red light I was aware of only after the screech of another car's brakes, I drove around deciding to face her. For a while I was thinking: Run, Macky, run for the Arizona line. Run away from her and what you two have done together. Run away and change your name and get a job sweeping up or doing dishes or picking lettuce and don't ever tell anyone and in fifty years when you're done and lying down that last time maybe then you won't have a nightmare. Maybe by then you'll be over it. But probably not and the hell with that idea. That was slow death, and if I wasn't going to make it, I wanted to find out fast. Newspaperman didn't have time for a slow death. Anyway, I had to stick around to see how the story came out. Yeah, more of that: Get down, Macky.

Alice had on the ten o'clock news, the same we'd just rammed into tomorrow's *Morning Mistake*, condensed and hyped even more. She got up and looked at me and knew right away. Her face went blank. She reached out and showed me a cassette tape. She put it in the answering machine and pushed the play switch and it was the one — Rissler and I sandbagging the Judge. I switched it off.

"I didn't do it just for that."

She kissed me. I held her, kissed her on the crooked spot on her nose and whispered, "It was your father who broke it, wasn't it?"

"Yes, Macky."

"You said he wasn't so tough. He was, though, wasn't he?"

"Yes."

"Those things you told me, about what the Judge did to you, that was really your father who did them?"

"Don't think of me like that, Macky. You saw the evidence."

"Who?"

"Macky!"

I bent her back and grabbed ahold of her hair. I let up, my arms around her. She waved her head back and forth.

"My name is Malone now. Alice Malone."

"So you changed it. That's all you can change."

"I don't lie. My father wasn't the only one. There were others. The Judge the last one. The very last. Now it's you and you won't hurt me, will you?"

"I'll try not to, Baby."

"I end up with men like that. You break the habit. Break it for me, Macky."

We held each other. She turned her face so I couldn't see it. "I remember his hands," she said. "One of his fingers had been cut off at the knuckle and it was all callused there and he used to poke me with it. He did a lot of yard work and his hands were strong and they seemed huge to me, because I was so small. I was scared of those hands, and I loved them. I lived with them for years. It got worse, and then I had to do something. He tried to block it with his hands and I blew one of them right off at the wrist. The right hand. I didn't mean to, but he tried to block it. He fell and his left hand was perfectly all right except for missing part of the one finger and I looked at it until it stopped moving. It's a story I tell. I told the Judge and he had them put me away and give me the cure, pills and TV, pills and TV. When I got out I went to talk

to him about it. He shouldn't have let me off. I told him that.
I should have been punished. He was very nice at first. He
helped me get a fresh start only it wasn't, because you never
can get one, can you? He sent me away to school and that
wasn't any good either. He got me jobs up in Laughlin, my
kind of town, everybody passing through and looking to
score and nobody knowing anybody else or wanting to. Then
he turned into another one of them, and his hands turned on
me like all the others. They were smaller, and not as strong,
but just as one hundred percent certain. I had to do something about them too. You understand how it was, don't you,
Macky?"

I told her I did understand, and I was just beginning to.
The ground had opened up and my guts were still falling.
Black and getting blacker. I started to laugh again, and she
dug her nails into my back. "Shut up."

"The fucking Judge! I keep seeing new angles on what he
was thinking, out there with the snakes. The only time he
ever cut anyone a break in court was with you, and then you
come back at him like this."

It would have made a good photo, shot looking down, the
two of us holding each other and laughing like people who
have nothing whatsoever to laugh about. It was one of our last
real moments.

I broke open the cassette tape — which all this had been
about, only it hadn't — unrolled the little reels and burned
the tape. I burned the microfiche on Alice Delgado too. We
went to bed and made love — I could still call it that! — then
lay there waiting. Later that night I must have fallen asleep,
because I had a dream that began with the chickens we'd
seen at the fair shitting on a checkerboard, shitting on my
square, and then all the rattlers lunging and lunging at the

Judge until his face swelled up and blackened and turned into Rissler's and began to burst. I woke up sweating and not wanting to go to sleep again.

Of course the combine wouldn't give us any respite. Rosie rousted us just after dawn. She kept knocking until I answered the door. She had the rolled-up copy of the paper off the porch but dropped it when I shoved her against the jamb.

"Don't rip the shirt," she said.

She pointed to the paper. "That's why it's the *Morning Mistake*. We never get it quite right. Is Alice around? She'll want to hear this too. It's about stolen rattlesnakes."

"Who cares?"

But I let go of her and closed the door on the neighbors while Alice wrapped herself in the sheet.

"You look better in person than on the eight-by-tens," Rosie said. "Maybe better isn't the word."

"Do you have something to say?" Alice said.

"You tell me. Yesterday I had a message from a guy I know in Game and Fish. I didn't get back to him until late, after deadline. He's got a snitch who's got an interesting rap. Seems there's this sleazebag west of town who deals in illegal snakes and lizards and coyote pelts, shit like that, and he's running around trying to figure out who broke into his place two days ago and snatched a couple dozen rattlers. Sleazebag couldn't take it to the cops, but he asked around, and this snitch passed it on. Guy named Cheney. Ever heard of him?" Beat. "Oh yeah, didn't you go out and shoot him one time he got busted?"

"Yeah. I remember him."

"I went out there and woke him up, thought I could catch him off guard. In person, he isn't the smartest. He wouldn't say doodly, but he's missing some rattlers."

"So write up a bright."

"It's the sort of thing that gets my journalistic instincts going. I spend all day yesterday on a story about a guy who gets bitten to death by a batch of rattlers, and then it turns out this other batch was stolen just before it happened." Another beat. "I can't help wondering if they weren't the same batch. Like, somebody stole the rattlers and put them out there where the Judge would be hiking, set it up some way. You see what I'm thinking?"

"Yeah, I see it."

"It's been your story up until now. Got any theories?"

"No." But I had to act like a journalist. "It could be worth checking around. If you need me to shoot something, Cheney or this snitch or another batch of rattlers, let me know."

"I'll do that." Then, to Alice, "What about you? You got any theories?"

"No."

Rosie walked over to the bed, inspected the tangled spread, our impressions on the pillows. "I hear Dunlap down at the prosecutor's is going after your phone records. He still thinks there's something in what the Judge said, about being set up the night Rissler got killed. Dunlap can't nail the Judge for anything now, the rattlers did that, so he wants you, Macky. He figures one guy nailed is better than none."

Rosie fingered the spread. "What were you looking up in the rag's library last night? You swiped one of the microfiches. A name file on somebody that begins with D. You looked through the Judge's files too. What's the tie-in?"

"Just a lead that didn't pan out."

"You aren't going to tell me?"

I could see where we were going. Best to say nothing.

"I looked through the Judge's files too," Rosie said. "It took me a couple hours. There was this wrap-up of some of his big cases, and it mentioned this one, that had to do with this Alice Delgado. Then I remembered the little girl who gunned down her dad fourteen years ago and got off on the insanity defense. There was nothing else on her. I thought there might be a fiche, but there wasn't."

"Another Alice," Alice said.

"Yeah," Rosie said. "You got any theories now? What were you doing yesterday morning about this time?"

Alice walked over to Rosie and bit her nose. As they struggled I slapped Rosie's pockets for the tape recorder, ripped it off her and the wire to the microphone inside her shirt.

We threw Rosie out. From across the street Suzy Kino was shooting us with a long lens. Rosie stood defiantly in the yard, rubbing the teeth marks on her nose. "I'm getting this story."

21

I HAD TO BE realistic. I didn't think we would make it. But when you get yourself into something like this, any chance at escape, no matter how impossible it looks, you have to try. And helping you along is the rush, only now it's from knowing there are no more rules you have to follow at all, except to get away. That's about as close to free as anybody can get anymore. Yeah, they were closing in on us. Pretty soon Alice and I were going to be back on the front page, and not in any way we wanted. The law would come after us then, but not until then, because no journalist like Rosie was going to turn over anything she had except under a big headline and in column inches galore. So we had a little time. I started packing.

"Mexico, I take it," Alice said. "Why is it always Mexico?"

"Because it's handy and cheap."

"The Judge used to go down there. He took me a couple of times. Down on the beach. We're going to make it."

It was worse with her acting sunny. I carried our bags out to my car and Suzy Kino was still shooting me. She was positioned behind her little red car peering her lens over the roof.

"Hiya, Macky," she said.

I went back inside and got the keys to Alice's pickup and went out and fired it up, belted myself in and then rushing wheeled around flooring it, smoking the tires, crashed into Suzy Kino's car, backed up and crashed it again, pinned it against the curb. When things slowed down I saw her scrambling away shooting me. I set the emergency brake and locked the pickup and got into my car and when Alice jumped in we drove off. It was making a nice sequence for Suzy Kino.

"See if anybody follows us," I told Alice. "Rosie wouldn't pull in too many on it."

"It looks okay."

Maybe to her it did. I wanted to keep flooring it and put everything and everyone behind us but that's one sure way to get caught, so I kept myself under control and even got it together to make a stop, at a bank branch, where I had to wait in the usual line. I took out everything in my checking and savings except for fifty bucks so I wouldn't have to do the paperwork on closing the accounts or argue about any outstanding checks, then drove us out to the interstate and south toward the border, Arizona's safety valve. I kept it to five over the limit and we made the Nogales crossing. The guards on our side waved us through, but on the other side we had to get out and wait, one of the main occupations down there, in an unfinished unwashed office with a dozen mismatched desks shoved here and there, only three of them being used, by bored men in ill-fitting uniforms and ill-fitting mustaches, only one of them showing any interest in the long line of gringos waiting, the way all gringos wait, with great overconfidence and queasiness because you never know when they'll pull out the little machine guns — don't get me wrong, I can see it from their angle too, why shouldn't they? Finally it was our turn, and the one processing the line worked us through the questions about where were we going and for how long and looked at some ID and accepted the ten spot to speed things along, which by then wasn't even laughable. Then with two fingers but surprisingly fast and with no mistakes he typed out the forms and one of the bored but idle ones came outside and pretended to look through our car. Another five spot, then we were officially okay for a while in Mexico.

"I guess this means you won't be getting the Pulitzer," Alice said.

I never liked to travel. Because wherever you get to, it'll be rigged, every place is, and in a strange place you won't know how they're doing it. It takes time to figure out, and coming in unconnected you might not be able to. At least at home, you know the basics. You know the most obvious lies and who to get in with and how much things really cost, and most of all, what you can get away with. Or at least, you have a better handle on it. So just crossing the border, no, that didn't give me much relief. With all the different factions of Mexican police and *federales* and other bandits, they could stop us anywhere, anytime, for any reason or none at all. They like to put up roadblocks to harass their own citizens, and gringos are just bigger game. How it comes out depends on which ones happen to be running things in that spot at that particular moment and what mood they're in, which is all the system they have down there, enforced by the little machine guns. Mexico is like Arizona, only worse.

I drove us south through the city that backed up against the border, slums of shacks crowding the narrow valleys and looking down on them from the hills, mansions with graceful archways and iron bars guarding every window and door, and spike-topped iron fences all the way around. Out into the

country, which was just more desert, now and then along the
road there were people walking, people with nothing a long
way from anywhere. The road was clogged with vegetable
trucks farting at twenty miles an hour, semis and buses
rocking along a little faster, blocking up miles of cars whose
drivers were so fed up they'd try to pass on an uphill stretch or
around a blind curve, which is all the roads down there seem
to consist of. Every man drove with his dick and the women
matched them. Outside of every little town the local outpost
of the Mexican Red Cross displayed some awful wreck out
front, as a warning about what one slip meant.

Six or eight hours of that was all it took to make the coast
and a place where it looked okay to stop your car without too
big a risk of it being broken into or heisted or taken over as
housing for three families and their goats: San Carlos, cactus
coming right down to the beach and hotels where gringos
came to play and have adventures. We got a room that opened
onto the beach and smelled of generations of disinfectant and
whatever hadn't quite been disinfected. The sun was setting
over the water. The swaybacked bed looked more tired than
we were, and when we lay down with our clothes on we saw
the black spots on the whitewashed ceiling where somebody
before us had swatted flies.

Alice's line: "I guess the maids never look up."

We had a couple of weeks of simulated escape, eating the
local food and drinking the tequila and risking the water and
the beach. My dogbite healed in the salt water. My other
wounds lingered, and my nights were ruled by dreams, especially the new one: the Judge's face swelling and turning
black. I always woke up wet with sweat, knowing it hadn't
ended yet. The hotel had the Tucson papers trucked in, and I
checked them every day for specifically bad news.

"Anything?" Alice would ask me.

"No."

"Maybe they'll forget about us."

"They won't forget. They're still digging, looking for proof. They're holding back what they have so far because it'd make them and their whole operation look bad."

"So maybe they won't print anything."

"And maybe you and I will live happily ever after. They'll use it if there's any chance they'll get beaten by the competition, or the law. Or they might use it just to clear themselves. Newspapers love to admit mistakes. It makes them seem so right. Mostly, it's just a hell of a story, a golden opportunity for everyone working on it."

"So we won't live happily ever after?"

"I don't know, Baby."

You go around imagining all the ways they can nail you. They might find some of our tracks that we hadn't managed to brush out, or a hair or fingerprint or speck of dirt in the wrong place. They might find the remains of the pit bull, Devil, and the bat I'd used on him, or our rattlesnake sacks. They might even be able to tell that the rattlers that had been stolen were the ones that did in the Judge. For all I knew, every rattler in Arizona was labeled as part of Operation Identification.

I couldn't talk this over with Alice, not in any serious way, because she was either acting like a giggly kid again, or like she wasn't there at all. We weren't talking anything over, or even making love with our eyes closed. We hadn't done much of that since, well, since the Judge got killed. That's how I had to think about it. He just got killed, that's all. And now we might or might not get caught. That was it.

I could talk it over with myself. I could have an interesting conversation with Macky about how little I really understood. She'd read me correctly all along, and that had made me trust her more than I should've. For too long I'd been understanding things the way a journalist does, in little snatches and snapshots, getting only as much as you need, and making sure it's usable. If I haven't described enough about all this, about everyone involved, that's why. So the Judge wore a certain style of shoe on Tuesdays and Rosie had a great recipe for corn muffins and maybe a lot of other people involved had to make do with two-wheeled trikes when they were kids. Whatever little things I understood didn't matter anymore, because all of us were faceless now, just characters in a story, some of us running the combine and the others running from it. For Macky, it was entirely too late.

I'd go out to the beach and run. That's about all I could manage. I'd run until I had to walk, then run some more and end up back where I started. I'd be out, way out over the gulf or up there with the sun or the gliding seabirds, or down there with the grains of sand that gave just a little under my bare feet. I'd be anywhere but where I was every moment I wasn't running.

One afternoon I shouldn't have stopped. I came back to the room tired, wanting to prove I wasn't, to the balcony side, which was just a deck raised a little by the drop of the beach. For the first time since it had happened, I was feeling pretty good, thinking maybe it might be history and we'd get over it. Of course that set me up just right to find out the opposite. I did a little chin-up on the railing and swung over and came in through the sliding glass door. Maybe I surprised her, and maybe I didn't. I smelled the burning.

Her back to me, she was sitting on the edge of the bed in a handwoven white cotton shift she'd bought down there. They make any woman look like a virgin, so the shops are full of them. She had the shift unbuttoned and swept behind her, and her head was bent forward in concentration. Smoke curled up from in front of her. All of a sudden the last place I ever wanted to be was in that room with her. I had to walk around the bed and take a look. She must have heard me. She was naked under the shift with a cigarette going and the hot tip pressed against her belly. She pulled the cigarette away and dragged on it to keep it glowing, and selected another spot higher up and pressed it there. This time I could hear the little sizzle, and smell that awful smell. She was stubbing me out along with that cigarette. She had six or seven new burns to go with the three scars she'd said the Judge had put there. That's what she'd said. *Said.* The journalism unit.

She dragged on the cigarette and looked at me from a long ways away and pressed the cigarette against her forearm. Alice the skull. It took me a while but I sat down beside her.

"The Judge never hurt you, did he?"

She dragged on the cigarette, tossed back her hair, and found another spot that needed burning.

"And your father?"

"Everyone's too nice to me. I'm so bad. I killed my mother, you know. I should be punished."

I grabbed her wrist and got the cigarette and crumbled it.

"Don't be too nice," she said.

"I'll try."

"I've got something to show you." She reached in between the mattress and the box springs and slid out an envelope, the kind the Mexican photo shops use. "Here."

The only thing harder than opening that envelope would have been to not open it. Of course there they were. Standard black-and-white three-by-fives, a little overexposed and poorly framed but clear enough. On top was a shot of me out in the desert standing over the Judge's body and the rattlesnakes. More shots like that, some framed tighter of me with the body. Shots of me batting down the pit bull, Devil, and lugging out Devil's body. She'd shot a roll on the murder.

"What do you think?" she asked. "Should I have gone with color?" She giggled. "I used that tiny little camera you used on the Judge. It wasn't very hard to learn how. You made it seem like you had to be an expert. I guess I've been hanging out with you too long. I got the idea nothing happens unless you get a picture of it."

She held up another of my cameras, a full-size 35 mm, and shot me. "I like the look on your face."

Yeah, Macky, get all the way down. There was a bottle of tequila and she shot me having some. After a while I made her have some and shot her and her new burns. The angle of the sun got lower through the lens.

Maybe you think I should have killed her right then. I thought about it: just locking my hands around her throat and squeezing. It wouldn't take too long, and she wouldn't fight it. But no, that would've been too nice for both of us.

I had to hold off so she could finish the story, snuggle up to me and tell me in that dreamy voice, "Silent one. I mailed a letter to the Judge today. I wrote out a full confession. He'll know what to do with it. I put in that shot of you with his body. It was so funny and you were so bad. They'll have to punish us now."

I let the tequila punish me. Of course pretty soon I had it all worked out, because there was still the slightest chance. I'd have to chase that shot down. She was crazy enough to have sent it. I had all the negs. I'd take them and the prints and leave first thing in the morning to get up there and intercept the mail, then cut back south across the border and cash in the car and get some fake IDs — they probably sold them on every corner in Mexico, or in special booths in the

big Sunday markets — and I'd keep moving and maybe there
was no extradition. Maybe no charges would be filed because
what did they have on me anyway, except maybe I went a
little too far to get a story? Yeah, I still had a chance.

I nodded off to that tune and came to in the dark. The
pillow next to me rustled. I reached over and felt something
scaly that moved and I jumped up and switched on the light.
It was a big black snake, not a rattler, a Mexican one I didn't
recognize, coiled up there on her pillow flicking its black
tongue at me. Is that primitive enough for you, Macky? Who
knows? Maybe she ordered it from room service.

She was gone. I was glad of that, and then I wasn't. Down
by the water she was screaming. From the balcony I watched
her performing for two flashlight beams aimed by the security guards who patrolled the beach. "He burned me. He
burned me." The flashlights aimed my way and swept closer.

The laugh split me open. I had the photos of myself doing
murder and I had the snake and I had her. I wasn't going to
explain my way out of a rap like that in Mexico, where all the
women are virgins. I ducked inside for whatever important
things I could grab and as they circled around and beat on the
front door I dropped over the balcony railing. I started what I
was good at: running.

22

I HAD ONE LAST LITTLE JOB in Arizona. It took me all night and the next day to reach the border. I rode the last leg in a melon truck, back in the bed with a bunch of *indios* who would've made a great photo spread. I took a couple shots of them with the camera that had ended up strapped around my neck. Newspaperman, yeah.

Nogales didn't look any better. I wandered around until I could sneak through one of the handy semipermanent holes cut in the border fence. Two kids lugging backpacks reeking of reefer ran through just before me, and just after came a dozen of all ages headed north to the fields to be pickers. It was two A.M., the Arizona rush hour.

Of course the Border Patrol rolled up and crackled orders to halt. All of us scattered and they came after us. I ran until I couldn't, then collapsed on the curb by an all-night plastic-food place lit up in orange and red. Get it up one last time, Macky. Go in past those lights and get that plastic coffee and the simulated food and get cleaned up and get ahold of yourself. I had money. I'd be all right while it lasted. Sure I would.

What the hell was that noise? Loud and piercing it came

around the corner of the restaurant: a man with one of those
blowers strapped to his back, whooshing leaves and dirt and
trash off sidewalks. That's what we do with our trash in
Arizona, hire somebody to blow it a few feet away, then
somebody comes along a little later and blows it back. He got
close to me and I jumped up and found the switch on the
thing and switched him off.

"Hey," he said. "What's your problem?"

"You got change for a dollar?"

He gave it to me and I went inside the lobby and bought
both Tucson papers out of the racks.

Of course those were the editions I'd been waiting for.
PHOTOGRAPHER SUSPECTED OF RATTLESNAKE MURDER.
FATHER-KILLING GIRL GROWS UP, SOUGHT FOR QUESTION-
ING. PROSECUTOR VOWS JUSTICE. And so on. Rosie had the
byline on the copyright story in the *Morning Mistake*. I could
see how she'd handled it, leaked what she had to the law,
prodding the official investigation that she could use as her
news peg. It's done all the time. I had to admire the front-
page shots of me ramming Suzy Kino's car to begin the
getaway. The *Evening Error* had wanted the sequence bad
enough to credit the competition. After that it was neck-and-
neck to see which paper could trash me and Alice the most.

I had to smile, reading it.

Arizona welcomes you back, Macky.

Of course it was all cast as suspicion and nothing proved,
but the allegations were lurid enough and the story strong
enough that nobody would believe it wasn't entirely true.
They had all the background on Alice, stuff about her stay in
the mental hospital that was news to me. They'd been digging all right. They even had editorials about how the best
thing about journalism was how it cleaned up after itself.
Since it was the *Evening Error* and the *Morning Mistake*, they

had to have something wrong, and they did, mainly, even with all that, they didn't have half the story.

It was still my story and I'd better get it all down. I went inside and took over a booth and started writing on the back of a paper placemat. I collected more placemats off the other tables and kept writing. The waitresses looked at me funny but I wasn't mumbling too loud or taking hostages so they just let me be and kept the coffee coming. The front of the placemats was the usual cartoon map of Arizona, with road-runners and all the sights pointed out. On the back was my story, the one you're reading. I got it all down and folded it up and put it in my pocket with the photos that would back it up, the photos they hadn't mentioned but would love to get so they could drop all the allegedlies and go for the throat. Now the package was together and ready to go if the last thing that could go wrong went wrong.

So go do it, Macky.

Hitch a ride with the first one leaving the parking lot headed north, an old geezer who wants to drive ten under the limit in his shiny new sedan with the turbocharged logo.

There's nothing more ludicrous than a turbocharged gee-zer. Arizona is full of them.

Stretch your leg over to his side and stomp the brake and shove the geezer out, Macky. Get this thing going.

Yeah, now you're really moving.

Drive on into the night and maybe you should just keep on going but no, take this exit and this road and off onto the dirt and push it on the curves. You always could drive, couldn't you, Macky?

Yeah, you can do it.

Ditch the car and sneak in as the sun is coming out of hiding behind those mountains and it's getting hotter and sure you're thirsty again and dizzy and haven't eaten in a long while but that can wait, plenty of time for that once this is over.

The ranch looks deserted and it should because they said it was and newspapers don't lie, do they? Heh heh. The gate across the driveway is locked and there's a new no-trespassing sign and what looks like a dead donkey farther in that seems to be half eaten-up, and under another blanket of flies what looks like one of the pit bulls, half-eaten too, the dogs must've gotten loose and run wild. Don't think about that because the mail is jammed in the red-white-and-blue box by the road, and that's another sign this is going to work out fine. Oh yeah.

Look through the mail and it isn't there, you didn't really expect it to be this easy, did you, Macky? No, it'll be coming, today, tomorrow, pretty soon. It'll be an envelope with her confession inside but that wouldn't impress anybody as crazy as she is, and what you want is the shot that's the only proof anyone can have at this point. You'll get the shot and then you'll keep on driving and you'll just be another guy with plenty suspected against him and nothing proved and that's enough to make you a celebrity these days. They'll give you boxes of money to give speeches about it.

Lie out here, just you and the sun and the cactus and the other bad-ass plants, this is the last sweat Arizona will ever wring out of you. Hold that thought until the little postman finally comes in his little jeep with the steering wheel on the wrong side and leaves a handful in the box and keeps on going. Don't let yourself go down there right away, let it wait just a little while longer, you'll never be in a hurry again.

Now, open the box. An envelope from Mexico all right. Her letter paperclipped around the photo. You can laugh now, Macky. Yeah. You beat the combine.

Of course footsteps are coming down the driveway from the house. You better hide one last time but why bother?

"I've been waiting, Macky."

It has to be her. Of course it does.

She's got a paper sack that she dumps out in the dirt. More shots, just like the one you hold in your hand, dozens of them. Every one of Macky the murderer.

"I mailed them all over," she says.

Yeah, oh yeah.

She reaches for you and you've got nothing left but to take her hand. And it's totally fine.

You walk together into the desert. You're shooting her. She's stripping her clothes off again and you can see what she's done to herself and she's saying, "It's cool, it's so cool, do you feel it, Macky?"

There's never been a woman as ugly as the desert at noon.

Here come the dogs.